Lock Down Publications and Ca$h
Presents

I0666777

# Dying For Likes 2

## You Reap What You Sow

Written By
# ARYANNA

First Edition 2025

Printed in the United States of America

This is a work of fiction. Names, characters, places, and incidents either
are products of the author's imagination or are used fictitiously. Any
similarity to actual events or locales or persons, living or dead, is
entirely coincidental.

Lock Down Publications
P.O. Box 944
Stockbridge, GA 30281
www.lockdownpublications.com

Like our page on Facebook: Lock Down Publications
www.facebook.com/lockdownpublications.ldp

# Stay Connected with Us!

Text **LOCKDOWN** to 22828 to stay up-to-date with new releases, sneak peaks, contests and more…

Like our page on Facebook:
Lock Down Publications

Join Lock Down Publications/The New Era Reading Group

Visit our website:
www.lockdownpublications.com

Follow us on Instagram:
Lock Down Publications

Email Us: We want to hear from you!

# Dedication

This book is dedicated to Tay, aka Big Mama, because I love you like 90's-2000 R&B.

# Acknowledgements

First and foremost, all thanks go to God for blessings I can't even begin to explain. I thank Him the most for lighting my way in the darkness that is the world. I wanna thank all my family and friends that support me, even the ones that I no longer talk to because, in some way, you helped me become me. I wanna thank my little big sister, Mathias, because I don't know what I would do without you. Baby Marcus, your uncle loves you soooooo much! I wanna thank my fans! If you fuck wit' me like I fuck wit' you, then this is a 4life thang!

I wanna thank my oppressors for keeping their foot on my neck because you're the reason that I reread the speech Willie Lynch gave at Jamestown. His instructions to you slave masters was clear: Break their will to resist! When it comes to me, you've failed miserably at that though, and I'm thankful. Due to oppression, I was diagnosed with Major Depression Disorder recently, which helps explain why it's taking me longer to produce these classics for my fans, but quitting ain't in me. As Maya Angelou put it, Still I Rise!

I wanna thank my wife for the intangibles and the things I can't explain. Thank you for loving this nerd and for actually seeing me in you. I love you like my life depends on it (and it does). May we see forever for eternities to come.

I wanna thank my LDP fam because you *all* help keep this ship afloat. A lot of companies folded, but the game is ours!

# Chapter 1
## (July 2025)

I immediately slammed on the brakes, causing the car to slide to a stop in the rain. Ignoring the sound of blaring horns coming from behind me, I turned to Joy and looked at the horror on her face.

"When is your birthday?" I asked.

"Wh-What?"

"Your birthday. When is it?" I pressed.

"May 13, 2004," she replied shakily.

"Oh, fuck," I mumbled, immediately doing the mental math and not liking how the numbers added up. It never even crossed my mind that it could be a possibility that Joy was my daughter, but that was because I'd given Pretty Girl more credit than to keep my child away from me. I wanted to yell and scream that this was all a lie, but something was pulling at what was left of my soul, telling me that this ugly truth was karma's haunting laugh. Joy was probably my daughter... And she was *definitely* pregnant by me.

"Stuckey, you still there?" I asked aloud, not hearing anything coming from my car's Bluetooth that was connected to my phone.

"Yeah, bruh, I'm here. Just come back and I'll meet you in the alley behind the church."

"Just give me a minute to think," I replied, hanging up, trying to grasp what it all meant.

"This-This can't be happening," Joy said softly, shaking her head in disbelief.

"It's gonna be okay."

"How? How the *fuck* could this possibly be okay if you're actually my father, and I'm carrying your baby?" she asked with her voice raising in borderline hysteria.

"Joy, just calm down. The baby…"

"Man, *fuck* the baby!" she yelled.

Before I could say anything else, she'd opened the door and bolted out into the rain at a dead run. I opened my door, prepared to go after her, but my instincts told me that I'd only make matters worse, and that was the last thing that I wanted to do. I knew that she really hadn't meant what she'd said about the life growing inside of her, but she wouldn't see that until she calmed down. I could give her space to do that because I had more pressing business to tend to. I closed my door and stomped on the gas while cranking the steering wheel hard to the left until I'd spun in a one hundred eighty-degree turn. I made it back to the church within minutes, and I'd barely slid to a stop before I'd hopped out with my gun drawn. Stuckey came out the side door, dragging Pretty Girl behind him like a thoroughly scolded child.

"Hold up, bruh," he said, blocking me from raising my gun and shooting that bitch in the head.

"Bruh, she's lying," I said defiantly.

"I'm not lying, and you know it in your heart," she proclaimed.

"How the fuck could you not tell me that we had a daughter, Diamond?! Twenty-one fucking years and you didn't say shit!" I raged, feeling the warmth of death creep into my heart.

"If Ant would've known, he would've killed us… or at least I thought that he would've. I don't know how, but he's known the truth, and he still never treated her any differently," she said.

"Because you're his blind spot," Stuckey said.

It didn't take much to realize that my brother was making sense because only a nigga in love would raise a kid that wasn't his. I wondered if the diabolical side of Ant outweighed any genuine love though just because he'd known that it was *my* daughter that he was raising.

"How sure are you that she's actually mine?" I asked, feeling sick to my stomach for even having to have this conversation.

"I didn't run a DNA test, if that's what you're asking. I just know when she was conceived because it was the last night that we were together."

My mind flashed back to a stolen, sweaty moment on a dark side street not far from Pretty Girl's house. When my brain made the subconscious comparison between mother and daughter, I had to physically shake the image from my head to avoid being violently ill.

"Did you fuck Ant that night too?" I asked, struggling to breathe around the bile trying to rise through the maze in my stomach.

"No, Ant and I didn't start fucking around again until a few days later."

"So, that means that there's still a possibility that Joy is Ant's daughter," Stuckey said.

"No, it's not. Ant spoke with certainty, and he wouldn't have been so quick to let her leave once he discovered who the man behind the face was," she replied.

"Unless he was simply writing off his own daughter because I'd been with her. We both know that he's that spiteful," I reminded her.

"If that's what you need to tell yourself, then fine, but the reality is that your spiteful, petty, vindictive ass just ruined Joy's life – no matter how you try to spin it. Now, where is she, Nathan? Where the fuck is my daughter?"

"I don't know. She hopped out of the car and took off running," I replied.

"And you didn't go after her?!" Pretty Girl asked with her voice rising in anger.

"That probably was the smart thing to do given the emotional overload that she must be experiencing," Stuckey said, trying to be the neutral party in this shit show.

"You disgust me. I can't believe that I was ever in love with your bitch ass," she spat.

"You weren't in love with me. The dick was just good to you. As for this current situation, you better know that you share just as much blame as I do. Not only did you not tell me that we could possibly have a kid together, you tried to use her to beg for your life that night at the banquet hall when Ant tried to kill me yet again. You can keep your mouth closed but not your muthafuckin' legs, huh?" I replied with equal disgust and anger.

"Yeah, whatever, nigga. Just stay the fuck away from my daughter. I'll handle it from here."

"Only if you can find a way out of hell," I said, raising my pistol and aiming at her face.

"Bruh, don't…"

Stuckey never got the chance to finish his sentence before no less than ten rounds spit from the barrel of my Glock, turning Pretty Girl's face into my most ugly masterpiece. The hatred that I felt for her was so potent that even after her body dropped, I lowered my aim and dumped the rest of my thirty-round clip into her.

"Do you feel better now?" Stuckey asked sarcastically.

"A little but I'm sure that I'll feel a whole lot better once Ant is dead. Where did your people take him?"

"He's in federal custody," Stuckey replied evasively.

"I know that, nigga, so stop playing and tell me what the plan is to get this muthafucka."

"Nate, you need to calm down and think for a minute. Ant's going down for first degree murder because he shot Yah Yah in front of wayyyyy too many witnesses. That gets him at least one life sentence, which means that he's officially dealt with. You've got other things to worry about."

His words caused me to pause for a moment and take in everything that had gone down in the last hour. The part that my baby sister, Yah Yah, had played in all of the chaos was something that I hadn't wanted to face, and even though she'd betrayed me, my heart still hurt because she died too young. In my heart, I knew that she hadn't intended for anyone to get hurt when she'd set me up for the fake robbery, and she'd just got caught up chasing clout like the little nigga she was fucking. She died for nothing at the end of the day, and Ant had to answer for that on *my* terms, not through the flawed court system.

"We both know that Ant will still wield his power from behind any prison wall, which means that me and mine won't be safe until he's food for the buzzards. Either you're gonna help make that happen or you ain't," I stated, challenging him.

"Bruh, I've done everything that you've asked of me, but the director of the CIA is involved now, and I'm not bigger than him."

I knew that the anger that I felt toward my brother wasn't justified, but I felt it nonetheless, and it almost caused me to do some impulsive shit that I couldn't take back. Instead, I tucked my gun while pulling out my phone and aiming it at Pretty Girl's dead body before I began recording.

"Aye, Ant, they say diamonds are a girl's best friend... I guess you'll have to find a new one now. What's the score again?" I asked, ending the clip on that note.

"Are you realty gonna taunt this nigga?" Stuckey asked.

"Taunt, torture, it's all the same thing as far as I'm concerned. I'mma do what I gotta do to make sure every second he's alive to draw breath is a second of excruciating pain that he feels."

"And what about Joy? Are you trying to cause her pain too, or do you not realize that you just deaded her mom in order to get back at Ant?" he asked logically.

"All wars have casualties, bruh, and that's a lesson that I'm sure Joy learned a long time ago," I replied, quickly uploading the video to social media and letting it fly fast like good click bait should.

I could see my brother shaking his head out of my peripheral vision, but his disapproval wasn't about to deter me. Ant had robbed me of too much for him to simply get to languish away in some federal prison for the rest of his days, but I knew that if I truly wanted revenge, then I was gonna have to be *all in* on my guerilla warfare tactics.

"Stuckey, you're my brother, and I love you. For these reasons, I'm gonna tell you that it's probably best that you let me finish up this mission on my own. It's only gonna get bloodier."

"But how much blood is enough, Nate? Where will this end? Have you even thought about that? Have you thought about how you're gonna explain any of this to Shytavia or Peanut, or did you simply forget that you had a family before you started fucking with Joy?"

I felt my jaw clench, as my anger returned white hot and ready to destroy, but I kept it at bay because his words spoken were the unvarnished truth. I'd pushed all thoughts of my wife and son from my mind in order to fully embrace my demons, and now that line had been too blurred for me to look back and see it. I didn't have a good answer to any of his questions, but I knew that I owed my wife some hard truths sooner than later.

"When was the last time that you talked to Tay?" I asked softly.

"The other day. She doesn't go more than two days without calling to check on you. I can never tell her much other than the fact that you ain't dead yet, and before you go off and get yourself killed, I think you owe her an explanation."

I contemplated his words and the weight of their meaning, still not knowing how in the world I could make this make sense to my wife.

"Do you think that she'll like my new face?" I asked, feeling suddenly self-conscious.

"I'm sure that she would, but do you think that it's smart to keep that face now that Ant has seen it?"

"It don't matter what I look like, bruh, because him knowing that I'm alive is enough to make him use every resource he has to find me," I replied.

"You can go into witsec. All you gotta do is say the word."

"You know that real street niggas don't go into witness protection, but I want you to set that up for Tay and Peanut. I want them as safe as can be before I make my next move," I said.

"And what's your next move?" he asked, looking at me with great concern.

"It's better if you don't know... but I have no doubt that you'll hear about it."

I could tell by the look on his face that he didn't like the answer, but he wasn't about to push the issue. I dapped him up and then went back to my car. Before I pulled off, I hopped on Instagram to see if my little video had been viewed, and the fact that over 2,500 eyes had viewed it already was astonishing to me. This generation's obsession with immediate gratification was crazy, but it was now a tool in my arsenal of manipulation, and I intended to use it to the fullest. The rules to war were simple in my mind: I had to win by any means necessary.

# Chapter 2

(Joy)

My feet were moving by themselves, and I had no sense of direction, but all that I knew was that I had to get the fuck away from the nigga who called himself Angelo. I didn't slow down until I saw the sign for a Holiday Inn hotel across the street, and I quickly dashed out into traffic to get there. I looked over my shoulder a few times, but I didn't see Lo or his car, which filled me with relief and longing at the same time. I couldn't rid my mind of the images and moments we'd shared over the last month, even knowing there was a very real possibility that the love of my young life could be the same man who'd aided in my conception.

I came to a quick halt before I walked into the hotel's lobby, and I vomited in the bushes next to the door. Once the wave of nausea passed, I stumbled inside and got a room using my emergency credit card that was on a micro dot imbedded under the skin on my right thumb. The card had been a gift from the man who I'd thought was my dad for my eighteenth birthday and using it made me think of him and the lifetime of lies I'd been told.

By the time I actually got into the room, I was so overwhelmed by my thoughts that I only had the energy to collapse on the queen-sized bed. When my head hit the pillow, my tears began to pour faster than the rain drops outside my window, and I was helpless to stop them.

I cried myself to sleep in a way that I hadn't done since I was a child. When I woke up, it was dark outside, and I felt more than a little disoriented until all the bullshit that had happened earlier came flooding back to me in waves. Before I knew it, I'd hopped out of the bed and made a mad dash for the bathroom where I threw up again until it literally felt like my baby was trying to come up out of my throat. I could smell the sour sweat coming out of my pores, forcing me to strip out of my damp clothing and get in the shower. The hot water did my body some justice, but I still felt a chill that went all the way to my heart. It felt like there was nothing that could warm that part of me. Once I climbed from beneath the water's spray, I pulled on the complementary Terry cloth robe and tried to figure out what my next move would be. I wanted to call Lo so bad, but I knew that I couldn't because I had no idea what the fuck I would say to him.

No matter what the DNA truth was, I knew that I had to accept the reality that Angelo was definitely *not* the man that I thought he was. Our meeting in San Francisco hadn't been the fateful one of my fairytale that I'd thought it was. It had been all calculation in his grand scheme to get back at the man that he thought was my father. Our child wasn't conceived in love but rather a hatred so deep that I would probably never comprehend it. I could admit that there was really no one innocent in this situation except for me, and that made me hate everyone on some level because no one actually gave a fuck about my feelings. I laid back down with my thoughts still scattered, but this time, I wasn't granted the reprieve of sleep. Instead, my brain began to reanalyze every moment that Lo and I had spent together, looking for any signs or red flags that I should've seen in real time. When I didn't find any, I thought about the saying that people could only hide their true nature for so long, and then their true nature came out in little ways. Either Angelo was a true psychopath, or on some level, he did love me. I was unsure how to feel about that given everything that I knew now, but I didn't feel as stupid as I had a few moments ago. Maybe the truth was that he'd hatched this diabolical plan of his and then became a slave to his emotions, like so many of us had in life.

This theory changed nothing, but as my hands went to my stomach, it did make me question the judgement I'd made about the emotions that motivated my own child's conception. With that thought came the memory of Lo telling me that no matter what, he loved me and the baby, and I wasn't in this alone, right before we'd left for the funeral. I'd asked him then where that was coming from because the declaration seemed ominous yet sincere, but he'd downplayed the impending doom he knew was coming. He knew that everything was getting ready to come to a head because him and his people had designed it like that.

So, looking at his statements in that light, I could now believe with some certainty that somewhere along the way, he had developed real feelings for me. His actions at the hospital alluded to the same thing, but what did it all mean? Whether or not our love was real didn't matter because it was a love that was beyond forbidden if what my mother said was true. I needed to talk to her and get some straight answers to at least some of the questions rattling my brain.

I sat up and reached for the phone in the room, regretting my impulsive decision to jump out of the car and leave all of my stuff behind. I called my mom a few times without getting an answer, causing me to hang up with some relief at being able to postpone what was sure to be an emotionally charged conversation. Despite my lack of appetite, I ordered something to eat from room service because my baby still needed nourishment. He or she was innocent, and no matter what happened, I'd give my last breath to make sure that innocence was protected.

While I waited on my food, I turned on the TV, and the first thing that popped up was the news. Before I had a chance to hope that today's events had somehow been overshadowed by something else, the image of the church popped up behind the cute blond news anchor. I wasn't following the repot until I heard my mother's government name, and that caused me to turn the volume up.

*"...It's unclear how her bullet riddled body ended up in the alley behind the church given that the only reported shots came from inside the church and were allegedly fired by Mr. Troell. The press release from the CIA director is that this is an active investigation. Reporting live for Fox News, I'm Erin Headly."*

After hearing the news report, my mind was spinning with more questions than answers, and the question at the top of the list was who had killed my mother. It was a toss-up between Ant and Lo because both had highly motivating factors to want her dead. My heart hurt, regardless of all the dirt that my mother had done, and her death made me truly feel alone in this world now. I didn't realize that I was crying until I felt the tears landing on my hands, and I was surprised because I didn't think that I had a single tear left to shed.

The knock on the hotel room door snapped me out of my own thoughts, forcing me to get up and retrieve my food. Once I had it though, I couldn't imagine eating it, so I set it on the table and climbed back beneath the warm comforter on the bed. Emotional exhaustion pulled me into a fitful sleep, but somehow, I managed to sleep through the night because my swollen eyes didn't open up until after the sun had risen.

I had no intention on getting out of bed because I had nowhere to go, but my baby was kicking on my bladder like it was their favorite rubber ball on the playground. Once I'd relieved myself, I intended to lay back down, but the voice in the back of my mind whispered that I couldn't hide out beneath the covers forever. I needed to do something.

I found the hotel's complementary tablet in the nightstand, and I began to order me some essentials online to be delivered. When that was done, I rented a car, bought a one-way ticket back to San Francisco, and ordered an early lunch to replace the uneaten hamburger and fries from last night. My purchases and the rented Jaguar SUV wouldn't arrive for at least another hour, so I waited on my food to show up, and once it did, I devoured it like a last meal. I could tell by the way that my baby started kicking when I bit the cheeseburger that I'd been riding on empty, and by the time I finished, I knew that I was gonna need more sustenance sooner than later.

Before I got on some big back shit with the room service menu, I hopped back in the shower to wash last night's sweat off of me. The hot water felt so good and soothing that I lost track of time, and only the sounds of knocking on the hotel room's front door pushed me out of the shower.

Once I had the robe back on, I answered the door to find two men standing side by side, one holding out a key fob, while the other handed me a garment bag. I quickly signed for my purchases and closed the door. I'd only ordered one outfit with a set of undergarments and a pair of black stilettos. After slipping into the soft silk panties and bra, I put on the Polo jean shirt and matching jeans, and then I threw all of my old clothing in the garment bag with the intention of trashing them. Everything that I'd been wearing would only offer tragic memories if I were to keep them, and I didn't need that. I still had three hours left before my flight left, which meant that I could just chill in the hotel room... or I could stop being a bitch and figure out how to get some answers.

Suddenly, my inner monologue took on the voice of my mother, and I knew what I was gonna do because Mama ain't raise no bitches. Once I stepped into my six-inch stilettos, I left the room and headed down to the lobby where I found the black SUV sitting right outside of the front doors. When I was behind the wheel, I had to contemplate the most likely place that the man I knew as my father would've been taken. I didn't know a lot about cops, but I knew enough to know that the niggas who'd put bracelets on him in the church weren't regular police. They had to be Feds, and logical deduction told me that the Feds would more than likely use the federal holding facility in Petersburg. All it took was a few seconds before the address popped up on the truck's GPS, and then I was on my way.

Fifteen minutes later, I pulled up and hopped out, but once I got inside, it took me damn near an hour of begging and pleading before I was granted a ten-minute visit. While I waited on my dad to be placed on the other side of the bulletproof glass in the one person visiting room, I tried to organize the questions that I wanted to ask in my mind so that I could maximize my time. A few minutes later though, when he entered the room shackled and handcuffed, my mind went blank, and I could feel the tears forming in my throat. Based on the surprised look on his face, I could tell that I was the last person that he expected to see, but he sat down and picked up the phone anyway. It took two deep breaths before I got up the courage to pick up the receiver on my end.

"Joy, what are you doing h…"

"Are you my father?" I blurted out, unable to control my impulsive need for the truth.

"I… You really need to have this conversation with your mother."

"Mom's dead, or didn't you know that already?" I asked sarcastically.

The genuine look of shock on his face saved me the time of asking my second question, and it also told me that Angelo had probably killed my mother — or at least someone he was in alliance with.

"The only way that I'm gonna get the truth is if you give it to me, and I think that you owe me that considering that it was your actions in part that got us to this point. So, I'mma ask you again… Are you my father?"

I didn't know whether he was pausing for dramatic effect or not, but the look on his face was one that I'd never seen before. It was the look of shame.

"You've been my daughter from the moment that life was breathed into your lungs... But if your question is one of biology, then I can't give you any real answers. The truth is that I don't know if I'm your biological father or not."

"But you moved with so much callous certainty back at the church, and you were willing to let me go with Angelo," I said, looking at him skeptically.

"Joy, you know like I do that it wouldn't have made a difference what I said to you. Even now as you sit here asking for the truth, I can still see your love for the man you call Angelo, and it's honestly sickening to see. His name is Nathan Ty, and back at the church, I was simply playing on your mother's emotions. I'm not even sure that she really knew the truth about who your real father is, but she knew that she was fucking with both of us, and that was enough to make her fearful of your relationship with him. Or maybe just jealous."

"Something tells me that you suspected they were fucking too, and you never quite got over that betrayal, did you... Dad?" I asked, adding extra emphasis to my last word.

"It's not proper to speak ill of the dead, but yeah, I knew your mother was a whore. I'd just hoped that you didn't grow up to follow in her footsteps," he said, smirking at me with a look of utter disgust.

The man sitting before me wasn't the man who'd raised me, and I knew that because that man never would've looked at me like I was trash. To that man, I was his princess who could do no wrong, but to this man, I was the daughter of a whore and a whore myself. The reality of his feelings caused the last pieces of my heart to shatter, but I vowed not to shed a single tear in front of this monster.

"Have a nice life sentence," I said, standing up and dropping the phone, as I turned to leave.

He didn't call me to come back, and I wouldn't if he had, so my eyes stayed locked on what was in front of me, and I kept my feet moving. By the time I made it back to my rented

SUV, I could feel the silent tears cascading down my face, but I refused to give myself over to the emotions of grief and sorrow. I was tired of being sad and tired of feeling like the pawn in everyone else's chess game. It was past time for me to start making some moves of my own.

The first thing that I did was drive to the local library so that I could access their computers. I knew that time was of the essence, which was why I wasted none when it came to transferring all of my parents' assets into my name. I had no doubt that Ant had money hidden in different places, but I focused on the legal millions right now because I knew that was what he would use to try and buy his freedom. I knew that in case of emergencies, I was both of my parents' durable power of attorney, so after I used that to liquidate all bank accounts, I moved on to their stock portfolio. When that was completely under my control, I moved on to their real estate holdings all over the world.

It took me a little more than an hour to complete my task, and when it was done, I had just enough time to drive myself to the airport. When I arrived, my flight was just beginning the boarding process, so I got in line and followed the leader. I made it to my first-class seat, dropped into the comfortable leather chair, and closed my eyes, as I took a deep breath. Exhaustion overcame me, and by the time I felt the plane start to move, I was halfway between awake and sleep.

"You and I need to talk."

Part of me was sincerely hoping that his voice was nothing more than a figment of my imagination, but the fact that my heart was beating fast and I could suddenly sense his physical presence told me that he was very real. I opened my eyes and slowly turned my head to my left. His hand was extended with my clutch purse in it, which I calmly took from him despite my emotions going haywire inside.

"Talk? Okay. Well, should I call you Angelo, Nathan... or Dad?"

# Chapter 3

### (Nate)

"You can call me Nate and allow me to explain before you jump to any conclusions," I replied.

"Jump to conclusions? I don't have to jump to conclusions when you made it so easy to do the math equation, *Nate*. You were in a war with Ant, you used me to get back at him, and along the way, you killed whatever family members that you could find. Let me not forget the part where you'd fucked my mom before too and quite possibly got her pregnant. Is there anything that I'm forgetting or missing?"

"Yeah, the part where I fell in love with you. I admit that I started this thing between us with more than ulterior motives, but you made it impossible not to love you. Are you saying that you didn't feel the same thing for me?" I asked, looking steadily at her with my penetrating gaze.

She maintained the eye contact for a moment, and then she averted her eyes out of the plane's window, as we slowly lifted into the air. I didn't press her for a quick response because I knew that this situation was a far from easy one, plus we had a flight that would last long enough for us to hash out our issues. At least that had been my objective when I'd had Stuckey track her down.

"No matter how I felt or feel, it's impossible for either of us to ignore the part where my mother insisted that you were my biological father. So, what do we do about that?" she asked, turning back to me.

"I've been thinking about that, and honestly, I think that she was lying because it was the easiest thing to say in order to keep us apart. Did you get any straight answers when you went to visit Ant?"

I could tell by the expression on her face that my knowledge of her movements was surprising, but she recovered swiftly.

"No, he said that he really didn't know whether or not he was my father. He just knew that you and my mother were fucking back then. As far as he was concerned, my mother and I were whores cut from the same cloth, and he suggested that I get my answer from her. Did she tell you the truth... before you killed her?" she asked in a voice laced heavy with accusation.

I kept my expression neutral, while I tried to decide how I wanted to proceed with this part of the conversation. It would be easier to lie to her and pin the murder on Ant, but something kept those words from coming out of my mouth.

"Diamond said that she fucked me and Ant within days of each other, but I think that she'd always secretly hoped that her and I had created a love child just because she wasn't happy in her relationship with him. By that premise, her saying that I'm your father makes sense because if she couldn't have me, then you *damn sure* couldn't."

I watched as she evaluated my response, knowing that she was listening to the words I'd spoken as much as she was the ones that I hadn't given voice to. A rouge tear slid down her face, and she swiped at it angrily before turning her face back toward the window. When she pulled her phone from her purse, I didn't say anything. I simply waited. When after twenty minutes she hadn't turned back to me or uttered a syllable, I knew that I was gonna have to switch tactics.

"Listen, Joy, I sincerely apologize for dragging you into a war that realistically started more than twenty years ago.

The adults in your life failed you, and I definitely failed you, but I don't wanna fail our child."

She didn't readily respond, or even acknowledge that I'd spoken for a few moments, and then, after putting her phone in her pocket, she turned to face me.

"Our child? What makes you think that I still intend to have this baby by you?" she asked in a deadly serious tone.

I opened my mouth to respond, but no words came out, so I shut it again and tried to organize my thoughts.

"As a woman, you have the right to choose... and as someone who was ultimately innocent in the war waged between me and Ant, I think that you would understand better than anyone just how innocent our child is. If you don't protect the life growing inside you, how much will you regret your decision later?" I asked softly.

Her eyes instantly glossed over with unshed tears, and before I could stop myself, I'd reached out and took her hand. I was surprised when she didn't immediately pull away, but I didn't say anything.

We sat like that, trapped in our own world of thoughts and silent communication, for the longest five minutes of my life. Then, without a word, she released my hand and stood up before heading toward the back of the plane. I watched her until she got to the section in the middle of the plane which housed the first-class bathrooms, and right before she opened the door to go inside, she looked back at me. I couldn't read the expression on her face, but unless I was completely confused, she wanted me to follow her. I waited a few minutes, trying to decide whether or not I was crazy, but eventually, my curiosity won, and I followed in her footsteps. I tapped softly on the door, and suddenly, the sign went from occupied to unoccupied, which allowed me to open the door. As soon as I pulled it open and stepped inside, I knew that I hadn't misread anything because she was halfway sitting on the tiny sink with her pants and panties off.

"Wh-What are you doing?" I asked in a low whisper, making sure to lock the door behind me.

"Shut up and make me feel better," she demanded, spreading her thick thighs enough for me to get more than a glimpse of her pretty pussy.

My mind hesitated, but my body was already in motion toward her, as my fingers fumbled with my zipper. The time between me feeling air blow across my hard dick and my dick pushing inside her warm, tight walls could've been measured in milliseconds. I wasted no time melting into her, pushing her back up against the mirror while folding her up until her ankles were wrapped around my neck. By my second stroke, I could hear her pussy slurping at my dick, fighting to pull me back to her, as I eased out of her vise grip. The way that her eyes rolled up into her brain gave her a look of being possessed, and that shit only made my dick harder with need and desire. I was trying to take my time, but by my next stroke, I was pounding her pussy hard enough to have her juices spitting at me like an angry llama.

"B-Beat this pussy up, Daddy," she demanded, moaning, as she fought for each breath.

Her demands drowned out my sanity because I knew how dangerous her pussy was, but I ignored the warning bells rattling my brain. When my fingers went to her clit, I felt her whole body seize up in anticipation, and that made me fuck her both faster and harder. I worked her like my favorite game controller during a live stream, and within minutes, we were both cumming in low growls that sounded prehistoric in nature. Once my dick stopped throbbing inside her, she pushed me back and hopped down off of the sink.

"You can leave now," she said, turning her back on me, as she picked up her clothes.

Her words stung somewhat, but I chalked it up to her just trying to make sure we got away with what we'd just done. It was definitely illegal to fly the 'mile high club' these days. I put my dick away, straightened my clothes, and made a quick exit. I could tell by the look that the couple seated closest to the bathroom gave me that we hadn't been as quiet as I'd hoped, but they didn't look like they were gonna tell the air marshal. The flushed look on the white girl's face told me that she was turned on, so if her dude knew what I did, he would slide off with her and tighten her cute ass up real quick.

When I got back to my seat, I immediately ordered a double shot of Branson Cognac and reclined into a comfortable position. I was halfway through my drink by the time Joy rejoined me, and she ordered an orange juice with light ice.

"You good?" I asked.

"That's a dumb question considering everything, ain't it? Or did you really think that your dick was good enough to be the cure to cancer?"

Her words carried more than a hint of attitude with them, and it was thoroughly confusing given our quickie a short while ago.

"Did I do something to piss you off while we were fucking?" I asked, turning toward her.

"No, you just reminded me of how much I hate that I love you, but I understand that it's my fault as much as it is yours. You did enter my life with an agenda, but I still had a choice of whether or not I fucked with you, and that's a decision that I have to live with forever. That don't mean that I gotta like it – or you – but I'll endure whatever I have to for our child."

The feeling of relief that I felt at hearing her speak in a way that revealed her plans to keep our child made me wanna smile, but I hid the desire by tossing back the rest of my drink. It seemed pointless to apologize, so I just kept my lips shut and signaled for the flight attendant to bring me another double.

"I've got a question for you though, Nathan. What's your plan?"

"What do you mean?" I asked, looking at her.

"I've done my research on Nathan Ty... Businessman *and* family man. So, where do me and this baby fit into your perfect little world with Shytavia?" she asked, smirking.

I did my best to conceal the surprise I felt that she actually knew my wife's name, but I was getting a bad feeling in the pit of my stomach.

"I ain't figured that all out yet, but we'll make it work."

"Really? You must think that you got a couple white bitches from Utah or something, but I'll kindly remind you that you're dealing with Black women, my nigga. We don't do the sister wife thing. I'm bout positive that your precious wife don't know what all you've been up to out here in these streets," she replied.

"Be clear, I'm *not* 'bout to sit here and discuss my wife with you, but we can talk about you and I all that you want," I firmly stated.

The widening smirk on her face told me that she knew that she was pushing my buttons, and she was enjoying it. The delivery of my drink was a welcome interruption and distraction, which she gladly took advantage of by pulling her phone back out and tapping away on the screen. The part of me that wanted to admonish her about her insistent thirst for social media kept quiet, as I tried to figure out a way to smooth things over between us. The last thing I wanted to do was fight with her, and in reality, her questions had been fair ones to ask given the fucked-up position that I'd put everyone in. I needed to fi-non-nesse this situation as my man, Sufu Naji, would say.

"It's fair to ask whether you and our child will have as equal a part in my life as my wife and son, and I apologize for not giving you a straight answer to that question. I'm not sure how all of this will work out, but I promise you that it *will work*. I won't let you raise our child on your own," I vowed.

"Even if it costs you your marriage?"

"It won't come to that," I replied confidently.

"But what if it does? What if your wife makes you choose between the family that you have with her and the one that you purposefully created with me?" she persisted, looking at me closely.

Her question posed a possibility that I'd never allowed myself to entertain because I truly couldn't see my life without my wife. Keeping Ava and Marissa a secret was one thing because they were a part of my past, but Joy was part of my present. I'd had an affair in real time, and like Joy had just reminded me, I'd gotten her pregnant on purpose. Shytavia could understand me doing a lot of fuck shit in the name of waging war, but bringing an innocent life into the world wasn't an acceptable war tactic. I knew that would offend my wife's Christian sensibilities, not to mention the violation of our marriage vows. All of this meant that, realistically, I could lose Tay... So, the question before me was would I be willing to lose Tay *and* Joy by alienating Joy now?

"I can't abandon you and the baby, no matter what the consequences," I said, staring into her hazel brown eyes steadily.

She maintained eye contact for a few moments, and then, her attention went back to her phone.

"I guess we'll have to wait and see if what you're saying is true. I'm telling you straight the fuck up that I'm not about to be anyone's secret though."

"I can understand that. I just need you to understand that this situation is very delicate, and it has to be handled as such," I replied gently.

"Delicate, huh? Nathan, you've *literally* blown my life to pieces on every single level, and you did it with deliberate intent. So, kindly explain why your wife doesn't deserve the same treatment?"

Her question caused a cold chill to run through my body, and the look of unbridled maliciousness in her eyes told me that her intent was wholeheartedly to rattle me. The only question that remained was to what degree she intended to fuck me over.

"I suggest that you really take a second and think before you answer because if your rationale involves her being 'innocent' then I advise you to save your breath. You'll only piss me off," she warned calmly.

"That's not what I was gonna say. I just didn't see the purpose to adding more fuel to the fire, creating a raging inferno. In order for all of us to move on, we have to figure out how to coexist, and that'll be hard enough as it is."

"True... But you probably should've thought about that *before* you stuck your dick inside me. Don't get me wrong, it's good dick, and I appreciate it, but it's like my mama told me back in the day – good dick comes with bad consequences."

I had no idea what she'd meant by what she said, but it gave me a feeling of apprehension that I couldn't shake. She didn't say anything else. She simply went back to her phone, and I went back to my drink. We spent the remainder of the flight in our own worlds, almost like two virtual strangers sitting side by side instead of two lovers who'd recently fucked while flying the friendly skies. I wanted to force more conversation out of her, but my instincts told me that this would be more than just a bad idea.

By the time the plane started its descent through the clouds and smog of San Francisco, I'd decided to use all of my physical prowess to bend Joy to my will. Good dick had got me into this, and it would help me to continue to navigate the choppy waters as long as the women in my life were still feening for it. When we landed, I began to mentally put together a plan of wooing that would take us into the early morning hours, but before I could put it into action, Joy turned to me.

"Pull out your phone," she demanded.

I looked at her curiously for a moment, but I eventually complied with her abrasive request. She tapped her phone against mine, and I immediately saw the download of information taking place.

"What is this?" I asked.

"I figured that you'd want to be the first person to see the new content that I just uploaded to my OnlyFans account, especially since the whole account was your idea to begin with."

Something in the pit of my stomach told me that this wasn't about to be as innocent as she was making it sound, but it wasn't until I saw myself reflected in the airplane's bathroom mirror that I fully comprehended. I'd never noticed her phone, which had clearly been positioned behind me in the bathroom, but the images were definitely real. When I looked over at her, she stood up and gave me a beautiful yet completely devilish smile.

"By the way, Nate, I made sure to tag you in the post on all my social media platforms, and I personally sent a copy to your wife. Good luck with that."

# Chapter 4

(Joy)
(Two Days Later)

I took a deep breath and focused all of my pent-up emotions in one direction, and then, I purposely pulled the trigger on my AR-15. I absorbed the kick back with little movement, which demonstrated that I was getting used to the recoil, and my eyes stayed on the target. I emptied the sixty-round drum in a matter of seconds, shredding the paper target hanging up at the end of the gun range, and I could feel the smile tugging at the corners of my mouth. I lowered the assault rifle from my shoulder down to the table in front of me, and then, I pressed the button on the wall to bring what was left of the target back to me.

"You've improved quickly."

"I'm motivated," I replied, glancing over my shoulder at Danny, the tall white boy who ran the gun range. He chuckled while passing me two more drums, one holding sixty rounds and the other holding one hundred. I quickly switched out my empty sixty-round drum for another sixty rounds, hung up another target, and sent it downrange to get annihilated like the last one. In the hour that I'd spent in downtown San Francisco, I'd alternated my aggression between visions of putting bullets in Ant's face, and I found it more therapeutic than a shopping spree. I hadn't heard from Nate since the airplane because he'd immediately booked a flight back out, presumably to wherever his wife was to try and justify the unexplainable. Part of me, only a tiny part, felt bad for exposing him like that, but it was the least that he deserved considering everything that he'd done. Just thinking about how he'd played in my face still made me angry enough to raise the AR again, and within a matter of seconds, I destroyed my latest target. I wasted no time exchanging the empty sixty-round drum for the fully loaded one hundred rounder, but before I got to do anything else, I felt my phone vibrating in the pocket of my shorts. When I pulled it out, I saw a number that I didn't recognize, but I answered anyway.

"Yeah?"

"You need to return my money and assets," Ant stated calmly.

"I don't know what you're talking 'bout," I replied, smirking.

"Joy, I suggest that you stop playing with me because I promise that you're not gonna like how this plays out."

"Daddy, are you threatening me?" I asked, sounding wounded.

"No threats here, just a warning because I still like you."

"Anthony, ain't nobody scared of you, so please drop the tough guy shit. Secondly, you're about to do a life sentence, and since my mom is dead, I just collected my inheritance. What I'mma need you to do is stop acting like you ain't got money stashed in secret bank accounts and safety deposit boxes. Use that if you need commissary money or lawyer fees," I advised.

"Little girl, *stop* making me repeat myself and return my shit!" he replied aggressively.

I laughed out loud before I hung up without responding and put my phone back in my pocket. The average muthafucka wouldn't so blatantly antagonize Ant, but at the end of the day, I knew that he could only do so much, and he wouldn't do the most.

"Reload these for me. I'm done for the day," I said, passing the empty sixty-round drums top Danny. The one hundred-round drum remained in place since it was still full.

He complied with my request, leaving the room without a word. I pressed the button to bring the last target back to me and added it to my stack, which I put in my bag along with my AR-15. Once I was packed up, I met Danny at the counter to collect my other drums and settle my account for the day. With that done, I stepped out into the midafternoon daylight, intending to go get something to eat and go back to my condo. My mind was on Chinese food, as I slid behind the wheel of my black Toyota 4Runner, but suddenly, I got the feeling that I was being watched.

I immediately checked my surroundings discretely, but I didn't see anything out of the ordinary. Knowing just how crazy Nate was now made me take my AR back out of my bag and lay it across my passenger seat. He'd talked like he wanted the baby that I was carrying, but I knew that I'd set fire to his marriage with the video I'd released on my OnlyFans page, and that could very well make him come for my life. He might've been able to explain the part about us fucking, but I'd edited the video with my own monologue explaining that this was a special edition because I'd just found out that my partner was actually my biological father.

That should've turned muthafuckas off, but since I'd dropped that video, I'd picked up 1.6 million more subscribers. With the money that I stood to make off of OnlyFans, I didn't have to take another photograph or work a job period, even with the fact that I was splitting the money with Nate. While it was true that money didn't solve everything, I was betting on the fact that we were making tens of millions of dollars as sufficient reason to keep Nate from killing me.

I still kept my eyes open, as I started my SUV and pulled out of the lot. After driving for ten minutes without noticing anything out of the ordinary, I started to feel foolish, and I chuckled softly to myself over my own paranoia. I made it to the Chinese restaurant and went in to place my order. It wasn't until I was on my way back to my ride a short while later that I got the feeling of being watched again, and I almost made the mistake of brushing it off like it was nothing.

I caught sight of a seemingly innocent black, four door Hyundai Sonata headed in my direction. What made it stand out was the fact that it was traveling the wrong way up the one-way street that I was parked on in Chinatown. I quickly hopped behind the wheel of my SUV, but before I could pull off, the Hyundai sped up and slid to a stop at an angle, blocking my path. When I looked in my rearview mirror, I saw a gray Ford Expedition racing toward me with a nigga hanging out of the window clutching an AK-47 in his grip. The lack of movement from the car in front of me made the decision of who I needed to deal with an easy one, causing me to grab my AR and aim out of my back window.

I didn't hesitate to shoot straight through the glass, knocking the nigga with the AK out of the Expedition's window and causing the driver to swerve. I swiftly adjusted my vision to put the driver in my sights, and then I let off enough shots to cause the window to explode with his blood and guts. I then turned back to the car in front of me, blocking my path, making a split-second decision to open fire on it through my windshield.

I sprayed the broad side of the Hyundai until my drum was empty, and then, I quickly exchanged it for one of the sixty-round drums that Danny had given me. I didn't open fire again because I didn't see any movement from the car, so I started my SUV and rammed the bullet riddled Hyundai out of my way. I kept my eyes open for more people trying to bring a premature end to my lifetime. My mind was moving faster than a fly's wings, but I made sure to obey all traffic signals while trying to make an educated guess as to who had sent some hittas my way. I knew better than to put it past Nate, but the ambush was more Ant's style, and it was no coincidence that this happened not long after my conversation with him. My mind and emotions were scattered to the winds, and I knew that I needed to regroup before I made a fatal mistake.

I rode around the city for a little while, debating about whether or not my spot was still safe enough to call it home. Ultimately, it had been my parents who'd helped me find and pay for my condo, so there was little doubt that Ant would send some niggas there to wait on me too. The harsh reality was that San Francisco wasn't safe for me anymore, and that realization gave me a new destination to head toward.

I went to the airport and rented a car after parking mine in the long-term lot, and then, I transferred all of my belongings into the black luxury BMW 855i before getting back on the road. It took me a couple hours to make the drive to Los Angeles, but it was worth it because I knew that Ant's mom's house in Brentwood would be the last place that he looked for me. I'd visited the lady who'd loved me like a grandmother at her residence enough times for me to have memorized the code to the gated community as well as the code to deactivate the alarm protecting the house.

Once I was inside, I went through the house with my gun locked and loaded in my hands, searching for any intruders just in case Ant was more clever than I gave him credit for. Once I was satisfied that I was alone, I was able to sit down and really analyze what happened in San Francisco. I chose the living room as my place to mentally decompress, meditating with the lights off and the AR resting comfortably in my lap. I had to admit that I'd recently done things to provoke both Ant and Nate, but the more that I thought about it, the more sense it made that Ant had tried to kill me.

Obviously, I wasn't his little princess anymore. Before I could question how I felt about this development on an emotional level, my thoughts were interrupted by my phone going off. I pulled it out of my pocket and saw that my girl, Hannah, was calling me, and I answered.

"What's up, Hannah?"

"Are you okay?" she asked in a panicked tone.

"I don't know for real. I'm kinda just stumbling through life right now," I replied honestly.

"No, bitch, I mean are you okay? Did you get shot at or hurt by the muthafuckas who tried to take you out?"

"Wait, how do you know about that?" I asked, confused.

"Check your Instagram."

"Hold on," I said, pulling my phone down from my ear so that I could access my IG page.

The first thing that popped up was a video that I'd been tagged in by Danny, and when I opened it, I saw the scene that had played out in the streets of Chinatown a short while ago. I had no idea how Danny had gotten the footage, but he'd obviously recognized my SUV because he'd sent the video to me asking if I was okay. The posting had already gone viral with the hashtags #aintshitsweet and #wildwildwest with just over two million views and comments.

"Oh, shit," I said, shaking my head, as I put the phone back to my ear.

"That's what the fuck I'm saying! What the hell is going on, and who is trying to kill my best friend?" she asked, sounding more than a little concerned.

"It's a long story, sis, but I'm okay, and I promise that I'll explain when I get back in town."

"Where are you now?" she asked.

"It's better that you don't know, and I don't want you to go to the gallery until this shit blows over."

"I don't understand. Are you trying to say that I'm in danger too?" she asked.

"Honestly, I don't know, so it's best to lay low for now. I'll call you in a couple days," I said, disconnecting the call before she could bombard me with more questions.

I immediately went back to the video clip to view it again, checking to see if there was anything that could identify me. The tints on my SUV made it too dark to see inside, but the bullets spitting from my AR-15 lit shit up like Christmas. Based on the video alone, I knew that cops would pull the traffic camera footage, if they hadn't already, and they would easily track my SUV back to me. Undoubtedly, they would wanna question me, maybe even detain me, and it was too easy for Ant to put cops on his payroll, so there was no way I was sitting down with the local police department. The reality that I was faced with was that I was gonna need help sooner than later, and as much as I hated to admit it, I knew of only one person that I could turn to.

Suddenly, I was regretting my decision to torpedo Nate's marriage, especially because I knew that he could keep me out of Ant's gun's sights *if* he wanted to. I had yet to think of a reason that he would want to though. I pulled up his contact in my phone, but I couldn't bring myself to type out a single word because there was no real way to play nice after what I'd done. I mean, what the fuck was I supposed to say, 'Protect me, Daddy'?

In the end, I typed the only thing that I knew would make sense and be the truth. I wasn't naïve enough to expect an immediate response, so I decided to take a quick shower to wash the funk of fear off of me. When I went into the master bathroom, I made sure to bring my AR with me, along with the extra drum, sitting both on the sink while I ran me a hot bubble bath. After about an hour of soaking in the jacuzzi tub, I finally felt the tension begin to release from my body, and my thoughts cleared somewhat. Running on pure adrenaline for hours was mentally, physically, and emotionally exhausting, and by the time I got out of the bath, I was damn near sleep on my feet. I dried off and then walked naked through the whole house, cradling my assault rifle, making sure that all the windows and doors were locked and the alarm was set.

When that was done, I went back to my grandma's room and climbed beneath the thick quilt on her bed while lying my gun beside me like it was my lover. I thought that it would take me awhile to fall asleep, but before I knew it, I was knocked out.

The next thing that I knew, the sounds coming from my phone snatched me out of my sleep and had me struggling out of bed to retrieve it from my pants on the floor. When I squinted at the screen, I saw that it was already 4 a.m., and I had more than fifty notifications. I didn't focus on the notifications though. I braced myself the best that I could, and then I opened the text message reply from Nate.

Immediately, I felt relief and anxiety at the same time, both of which eliminated all traces of the good sleep that I'd been robbed of. I reread the message that Nate had sent twice before moving to put on my clothes, as my mind formulated what my next move would be. I went online and ordered a ride to come get me from LAX and take me *back* to the LAX, and then, I bought three different plane tickets to three different locations in order to confuse anyone tracking me. While I waited on the ride to show up, I gathered my stuff and put it back into my bag before going to the garage and throwing everything in the trunk of my grandma's dark blue Maybach coupé. After that, I walked through the house, looking for anything that might aid me, and surprisingly, I found 50,000 in cash in the bottom of my grandma's dresser drawer. I knew that she'd never really been a fan of banks because she didn't believe in people making money off of her money, but I hadn't expected to find this much cash on hand. I stuffed my pockets with $40,000, and when the driver pulled up to pick me up, I went outside and gave him $10,000.

"If anybody asks, you dropped me off at the airport. Understand?"

"Yes, ma'am," he replied readily, accepting the money and pulling off.

With that taken care of, I returned to the garage, climbed behind the wheel of the Maybach, raised the garage door, and slipped out into the night. By the time the sun had risen good, I'd made it to Las Vegas where I got something to eat at Burger King while I researched different car dealerships. I found an exotic car dealer off of the Vegas strip who would do a deal based on a trade in, and I contacted him so that he knew I was coming through with something of interest.

When I got there and he saw the pristine condition that the Maybach was in, he was only too happy to accept it as a trade for a silver Porsche 911 Turbo. I slipped him $10,000 to keep things discrete as well as to have the GPS locater chip removed from both cars. Within an hour, I was back on the road, and a few hours later, I was pulling up to a hotel in Denver, Colorado. I left my bag in the trunk because I didn't wanna show up on some bullshit, and then I took the elevator to the penthouse's suites. As soon as the door opened and I stepped out, three niggas in suits surrounded me with their standard issued Glock .40s out and ready.

"This area is restricted," one man stated.

"I'm expected," I replied.

My response caused one man to leave and enter one of the two doors leading to the penthouses, and a few moments later, a beautiful, red haired, white woman came out.

"Are you Joy?" she asked.

"Yes."

"Nate told me that you were coming and to keep you safe. My name is Marissa."

# Chapter 5

(Nate)
(North Carolina)

I could feel my heart beating in my toenails with every step that I took that brought me closer to the front door of the house where my wife and son were. It had taken me damn near three days to work up the courage to face her, and even now, I still couldn't do it without my brother with me like private security. When I finally got to the front door, I stopped, and it felt like my body had locked up because I couldn't even raise my arm to ring the bell.

"Move, pussy," Stuckey demanded, chuckling and nudging me aside, as he stepped in front of me and rang the doorbell.

I was grateful to have him by my side despite the merciless teasing he'd forced me to endure during the ride down here from D.C.

It had been my intention to come straight to my wife from the airport in San Francisco, but I knew her well enough to know that she needed a minute to chill, or she might accidentally shoot me on purpose. I'd flown back to the nation's capital and had Stuckey pick me up, thinking that he could help me smooth shit over, but all he'd done so far was laugh at me for getting played by a twenty-one-year-old. I couldn't deny that I felt more than a little stupid because I'd misread Joy badly, but that was spilled milk that I couldn't put back in the container. It was time to face the music.

39

"Mommy, door!" Peanut yelled from the other side of the solid wood structure.

A few moments later, I heard Tay's footsteps, and then, she was pulling the door open with my son on her hip. Her eyes went to Stuckey first, but then, they immediately slid to me, and I saw the fire light them up.

"Daddy!" Peanut squealed, reaching for me.

I'd thought that he'd need some time to adjust to my new face, but I knew that his mom had been showing him pictures of me for the last seven months because she had only thought I was dead for a little while until Stuckey explained the play to her.

I took a step forward to open my arms to him, but Tay shifted away from me and handed him to my brother instead.

"Take him inside, Stuckey," she said, stepping out onto the porch with me.

Everything in me wanted to tell that nigga not to move, but I kept my mouth shut because no matter what happened, I knew that I deserved it. Peanut called for me again, and I waved at him, as the door closed.

"Bae, before you go off, let me explain because...."

I never got to finish my sentence because Tay took off by hitting me with a two piece to the face. I instantly tasted blood in my mouth, but I was way more focused on blocking the follow up right hook that she was throwing my way.

"Baby, chill!" I pleaded, holding my hands up.

"Ain't no baby over here, bitch ass nigga, because you don't fuck with me for real."

"I do. I swear!" I replied, blocking another straight jab she'd aimed at my nose.

I could tell by the crazed look in her eyes that trying to reason with her wasn't gonna work, which left me with only two choices – either whoop her ass or run from her. I wasn't about to put my hands on my wife, so I jumped off the porch with my hands still up to show my surrender.

"Tay, I didn't mean for this shit to happen, I swear. I was just using her to get back at Ant and Diamond."

"Oh, let me guess, fucking her was the only way that you could use the bitch? The fuck outta here with the shit, you ho ass nigga! You just thinking with your dick as usual," she raged, coming down the porch steps toward me.

"I could've shot her in the face, but I didn't just wanna hurt Ant. I wanted to humiliate the nigga," I explained, still backing away from her.

"And you didn't give a fuck about humiliating me in the process, right? You made a fucking OnlyFans page with this bitch and put up I don't know how many videos of you two doing all types of freaky shit. And you want me to believe that you did *all* of that as some type of strategy? Shut the fuck up, nigga, because whether you've got a new face or not, I still know how you fuck a bitch, and you were *definitely* enjoying yourself with that ho! Even when you knew that she was probably your own daughter, you *still* fucked her... That's just sick," she said, putting her hands down and staring at me in disgust.

"She's *not* my daughter!"

"How do you know that? Did you do a DNA test, or was the pussy just so good that you were willing to overlook what's right in front of you?" she asked in sarcastic anger.

"Her mother was a habitual liar, and she was free with the pussy, so I'm not believing shit that she has to say."

"You know what? It don't even matter though because the bottom line for me is that you fucked the bitch. I told you from the jump that I don't play that cheating shit, and I meant it. We're done," she said, pulling off her wedding ring and band, dropping them in the grass beneath our feet.

Before I could go into my begging and pleading like a 90's R&B king, she turned and walked away from me, heading back into the house. I couldn't say that I was completely shocked by her response, but I couldn't lie and say that it didn't hurt my heart either. I really did love my wife, but I knew that I'd fucked up by thinking that I could love two women at the same time. The only thing that I could do now was pray that I could somehow change her mind in time because losing her like this just wasn't an option.

After I retrieved her wedding set from where she'd dropped it, I put the rings in my pocket and tried to decide what to do next. When the front door suddenly opened again, I expected to see Tay holding one of my guns, aimed at me, but instead, it was my beautiful baby boy running toward me. I opened my arms, and as soon as he got close enough, he jumped straight into them.

"Daddy, I missed you."

"I missed you too, little man. You got so big on me," I said, squeezing him tightly.

He giggled and pulled back so that he could look at my face. Using his tiny index finger, he traced the lines of my face, and I knew that he was marking the differences as he saw them.

"Daddy, what happened to your old face?" he asked, full of child-like curiosity.

"I had an accident and got hurt. It's okay though because it's still me under this new face."

"That's what Mommy said," he replied, nodding, as he took my head in his hands and brought us inches apart.

I paused for a few seconds, and then, I covered his tiny face with kisses the way that I always used to. The sound of his high-pitched squeals and laughter was a much-needed balm on my tortured soul, but it was bittersweet because in the back of my mind, I knew that I might've destroyed my family forever. I shook those thoughts from my mind though, as I put him on his feet and told him to go get his tiny Nerf football laying over by his mom's rose bushes. For the next hour, I blocked everything from my mind except for my son, and we played together happily in the front yard like today was a typical weekend. I could've done it all day honestly, but Tay stepped out on the porch and called him in the house to eat lunch.

I was debating on whether or not I should accompany him into the house, but he made that decision for me by taking my hand and pulling me along with him. I let him lead the way up the steps and into the house, but I stopped just outside of the entrance to the kitchen. Stuckey was already sitting at the dining room table, feeding his fat ass face with some mouthwatering BBQ ribs, but I saw that Peanut's plate had chicken nuggets with mac and cheese. The aromas from the feast that Tay was fixing had my mouth trying to touch my knees, but I knew better than to fix my face to ask for a plate of food.

Both food and cooking were a thing of ours, kinda like a love language that we spoke together, but it was also how she dealt with stress. The kitchen was her safe space when I wasn't or couldn't be, and I could tell that she was trying to block out my bullshit right about now. I wanted to whoop my brother's ass for being petty enough to eat my wife's cooking in my face. I knew that I had bugger problems to worry about though, and they began with the woman standing across the room in front of the stove. Even with her back to me, I could feel the anger that I was sure still contorted her beautiful facial features, and everything in me wanted to go to her and say anything I could think of for her to forgive me. Despite my desperation, I knew that no words would work right now.

"Daddy, come eat," Peanut said, holding up a chicken nugget in offering.

"I'm not hungry, little man, but you make sure that you eat all of your food," I replied, forcing a smile on my face.

He nodded as he stuffed the tiny nugget in his mouth, but my eyes flickered toward his mother, as I caught sight of her movement away from the stove. She went to the refrigerator and filled Peanut's cup with Kool-Aid before putting it beside him on the table, and not once did she look at me or acknowledge my presence. I was really struggling not to push the issue of conversation, even though it would inevitably lead to confrontation, but my attention was immediately captured by my phone sounding off from an incoming text message. I read the short message five times before I opened the attached video link, and what I saw presented a whole new problem.

"Muthafucka!" I growled angrily.

When I looked up from my phone, Stuckey was staring at me intently with a delicious looking rib paused in midair on the way to his mouth.

"Those sounded like shots from an AR-15... a lot of shots," he said, giving me a questioning look.

I could feel Tay's eyes burning a massive hole through my frontal lobe, but I ignored her, as I tried to figure out how to respond to Joy. All her message had said was that she needed help. The video said so much more though because if someone had taken a run at her in broad daylight then they *really* wanted her dead. Only one person came to mind when it came to suspects who would be so reckless, and just thinking his name made me grind my teeth.

"We gotta go," I said, giving my brother a knowing look.

"Right now?" he asked, looking down at the mountain of food still piled on his plate.

"My nigga, do it look like I'm fucking joking with you? Get the fuck up and let's go," I demanded, walking toward my son.

I gave Peanut a quick kiss on his forehead and whispered in his ear that I loved him and wanted him to be a good boy for his mom. He nodded his head because his mouth was busy working on the chicken nuggets. When I looked up, Tay was standing a few feet away, subconsciously fidgeting with the necklace around her neck, looking at me like she wanted to speak.

I knew that there was no way that I could offer any type of explanation that wouldn't twist the knife that I'd already put in her heart, and the last thing that I wanted to do was keep hurting her. For that reason, I didn't say anything, but I did pull her wedding set from my pocket, and I laid both rings on the table.

"I'll meet you outside, bruh," I said, turning to leave.

As I made my way back to my Dodge Hellcat, I sent Marissa a text message letting her know that I needed a huge favor before I gave her a brief explanation and sent her the video. I slid into the driver's seat and waited. A few minutes later, Stuckey came out with a paper plate in his hands, and by the time he climbed into the passenger seat, Marissa had replied.

"What's good, bruh? Who was shooting shit?"

"Joy," I replied, sending Marissa another text asking her for her address.

"Joy? The fuck she doing letting off shots like that?" he asked, chomping down on another BBQ rib.

"My best guess is that Ant tried to kill her," I said, texting Joy Marissa's address with instructions for her to go straight there and wait.

"Ant? Wait, you think that Ant is trying to kill the woman that he raised as his daughter without even knowing if she's his biological child first?"

"It don't matter if she's my kid or not because she's *pregnant* with my kid, and that makes her dead to him. I tried explaining to your simple ass that Ant wasn't going away and that he needed to die, but you didn't listen, and I almost lost my unborn child, nigga," I replied, looking at him with the side eye.

He was smart enough to keep his mouth shut because any comment would've made me dive on his muthafuckin' ass. Instead, I started the car and peeled out of the driveway with the single thought of killing Ant as soon as humanly possible.

"Where are we going?" he asked five minutes later.

"I'm taking you to the airport so that you can hop a flight to Colorado."

"Uh, what the fuck is in Colorado besides white women and snowsuits?" he asked, clearly confused.

"Marissa and Ava are in Colorado... And I just sent Joy there to hide out," I replied, glancing over at him.

"Oh, you're a *bold* muthafucka for that one, bruh."

"Nah, it's just the smartest move right now because no one knows about Marissa and Ava hiding out there, which means that Ant is in the blind for once," I explained patiently.

He was quiet for a minute, but I could see him nodding out the corner of my eye.

"Okay, but why am I going to Colorado instead of you?" he asked finally.

"Because I've got shit to do."

"Bruh, let me find out that you're about to throw me in the lion's den with all of these volatile women so that you can escape the shit show once Joy starts to tell her story."

"I don't duck no smoke, my nigga, but if you'd rather that I go hold hands with those volatile women while *you* do the killing, then just say the word," I replied, looking over at him with a serious expression.

"Kill? Who are you 'bout to kill now?"

"It's better if you don't ask me any questions," I warned.

He didn't reply, but I knew my brother well enough to know that there were big questions burning a hole through his BBQ laced tongue. I knew that he wouldn't ask though because I'd said enough for him to understand that him having plausible deniability was as important as whoever I intended to send to the afterlife. We rode the rest of the way to the airport in Charlotte, North Carolina in silence, no doubt making our own individual plans for the imminent future. When I pulled over to drop him curbside, he hesitated to get out, and then, he turned to face me.

"I know that you know how to handle yourself, bruh, but I wouldn't be a good big brother if I didn't tell you to be careful."

"I thought that we agreed a while ago that I was the big brother in this equation," I said, smiling crookedly at him.

"I'm serious, Nate. I don't know what you've got up your sleeve, but it's guaranteed to be dangerous and stupid. All I'm saying is that you need to think every move through, consider each and every possible fatal outcome, and create contingency plans for your contingency plans."

"I hear you, bruh, and I promise not to go off halfcocked and get myself killed. You'd probably kill your damn self just to avoid dealing with my baby mamas," I replied, laughing.

"Shitttt, you ain't *neva* lied," he said before he opened the door and climbed out.

With him on his way to handle the issues building on the West Coast, I felt comfortable turning my full attention to what had to happen out here on the east. I knew that the drive back to D.C. would take about seven hours if I did the speed limit, which gave me time to make my arrangements.

As soon as I got on the highway, I set the cruise control to one hundred miles per hour and engaged the autopilot feature, and then, I pulled out my phone to make phone calls. Darkness was coming to our nation's capital, and I was bringing a blood rain with it.

# Chapter 6

(Joy)

Walking into the penthouse suite, I wasn't exactly sure what to expect, but seeing multiple guns within easy reach put me at ease somewhat.

"Are you expecting more visitors than just me?" I asked, looking at Marissa, who'd moved behind the bar.

"No, I'm just expecting the unexpected. Ant has a bad habit of not knowing how to die or fight fair."

"You-You know Ant?" I asked, unable to conceal my surprise.

For a few moments, she just stared at me, and then, she went back to fixing her drink.

"Yeah, I know Ant, and I knew Diamond. I'm sorry for your loss," she replied.

"How did you know them?"

"I grew up with Nate," she replied shortly.

I could sense that there was a lot hidden in that statement, but knowing Nate, it was probably safe to assume that he'd fucked this beautiful woman.

"Tell me something. What happened that would cause Nathan to send you into hiding?" she asked, coming from behind the bar and taking a seat on the plush floral couch. I sat on the loveseat across from her and thought about how much I should say.

"How much did Nate tell you?"

"That's the thing. He didn't tell me shit except to protect you. On a good day, he's not the best at explaining himself, but him and I don't really do the cryptic shit because he knows that I'll fuck his ass up," she replied seriously.

"Sounds like we know two different men because the Nathan that I know is a professional liar."

"Ah, so the illusion that is good dick has worn off, I see. That's a start because you're gonna need absolute clarity when it comes to being in Nate's world. I don't know everything that's happened since I last saw him, but if he's protecting you, then he obviously let his feelings for you grow unchecked. Let me be the first to tell you that it's dangerous to be in love with him, but it can be even more dangerous to be loved *by* him," she said before taking a thoughtful sip of her drink.

"Sounds like you speak from experience," I replied, giving her a knowing look.

Her smile was instant and brilliant, and it confirmed my initial assumption.

"It's still crazy how one man can literally redefine the word *complicated*, huh?"

"Shit, tell me about it," I agreed, shaking my head, as I thought about my own experiences with the man that we'd obviously have to share.

"Believe it or not, deep down, he's really not a bad guy. He's worked really hard to change his life and leave the bullshit behind him, but when he was forced to kill those kids who staged that robbery, it pulled him right back into the world he'd fought to escape."

"I can understand that, and on some level, I can even empathize with it... but I can't agree with all of the moves and decisions that he's made since that situation took place," I replied.

"I understand that, especially because he took the lives of people close to you in the name of revenge. Not to mention the fact that he used you."

49

"I see that you don't pull any punches," I said, feeling somewhat irritated by her matter-of-fact tone about the things that had ruined my life.

"I'm sorry because I'm not trying to sound callous, and if it's any consolation, I did try to talk him out of all of this bullshit before he'd put the grand scheme into play."

"Maybe next time, you should try harder," I replied, feeling the anger building inside of me.

She let my comment slide by focusing on the drink that she was sipping, but the tension between us was obvious. It wasn't my intention to make this woman my enemy, especially since I was so short on allies, so I mentally checked myself and tried to focus on the bigger picture.

"I'm sorry. My emotions are all over the place, and it's affecting my thinking," I said softly.

"It's okay and more than understandable. Do you want a drink? It'll help take the edge off."

"I'd need a whole bottle for that, but... I can't drink," I replied, looking at her.

For a moment, she simply stared at me with a quizzical expression, but as I watched her, that expression suddenly morphed into complete and utter shock.

"You're pregnant?" she whispered, leaning toward me.

"I guess that he really didn't tell you anything about what's going on."

"No, I'm lost to most of what's happened in the last seven months, other than the news reports that I was able to connect to him just because I knew that his ultimate goal was to get to Ant," she said.

"Yeah, well apparently, I was a big part of that plan and so was getting me pregnant."

"Wow..." she said, clearly fucked up by my reaction.

Given that this woman obviously had history with Nate, I expected to see jealousy pop up in her eyes at any moment, but it didn't happen.

"I can tell that you're surprised that Nate got me pregnant, but I'm wondering why that surprises you," I said.

"A couple reasons but mainly because of his wife and son. If she finds out you're pregnant, I don't think their marriage would survive, so it don't make sense that he would do that on purpose, not even to get back at Ant. Why don't you tell me what I'm missing?"

"He says that he loves me," I replied somewhat nonchalantly.

"Okay, that's a safe bet, but there has to be more," she insisted.

I took a moment to think about exactly how much I should tell her, and I reasoned that this was obviously someone that Nate trusted, which meant that she didn't mean me any harm.

"Honestly, I think he believed that he could have it all, meaning me and his wife, once he'd gotten his revenge on Ant. It was the unexpected things that he couldn't control that ultimately put his marriage up for grabs. In hindsight, I do feel bad for what I did, but I was moving off of the emotional rollercoaster of feeling used, fucked over, and alone, so I just wanted to hurt him," I confessed.

"You speak as if you knew that he was married when you were fucking him."

"No, I didn't. It wasn't until I found out from Ant what his real name was that I started to dig into his past, and that's when I'd discovered that I'd always been a pawn in his game with Ant and my mom. So, naturally, I wanted some type of revenge or justice, but I didn't know how to get it until we were on the plane together. So, I fucked him in the bathroom, recorded it for my OnlyFans page, and then once I posted it, I sent the link to his wife," I said.

"You did *what*?"

The shock of my revelation caused her to lean closer and sit her drink on the coffee table in between us.

"Yeah, like I said, it wasn't my finest moment, and it was some petty, young girl shit," I conceded.

"Agreed but wait. Nate knows that you did all of this, and he *still* sent you out here to protect you? Part of me thinks he did that just to protect the baby, but something tells me that you're holding back a big piece of the puzzle so spill it," she demanded.

"Damn, are you a cop or something?"

"Actually, I'm the chief of police for Washington D.C.," she replied matter-of-factly.

"Chief of police... Wait a minute. When I was looking into Nathan's past, I found the video of you killing him in the alley after he kidnapped and killed your daughter following some fundraiser event."

"That's part of the story, but the reality is that we staged the whole thing after your father tried to kill *all* of us at the event he'd thrown in the name of Nate's mom, who he'd had murdered. Nate wanted to make me and my daughter invisible and get the advantage by making Ant think that he was dead," she said.

"Sounds like he went through a lot to protect you too."

"Nice try, but you can't deflect or make me forget my original line of question, so let's cut the shit," she said, taking a more serious tone.

I hesitated not because this cop inspired fear but because the uncertainty of the truth scared the fuck out of me. What if Nate really was my sperm donor? How would that affect the child that I was currently carrying? The fear of the unknown was completely justified, but deep down, I knew that I couldn't hide from the truth forever, no matter what else was going on around me.

"At my grandmother's and uncle's funeral was when Nate revealed his true identity, and my mom freaked *the fuck* out. At first, I thought that it was just because her and I had fucked the same nigga, but then she said some wild shit after we left... She told Stuckey that Nate was my biological father."

The way that her mouth hung open to her chest was comical, but I knew that this was far from a laughing matter. It wasn't even one of those situations where you laughed to keep from crying.

"There's no way you're serious," she replied just above a whisper.

"That ain't something that anyone would play about."

My response caused her to drain the remaining liquor in her glass, and then, she got up to fix herself another drink. While she was doing that, an attractive, light skinned female who looked to be around my age came up from out of the short hallway, yawning and smoothing her hair out.

"Damn, Ma, you having Cognac for breakfast?" she asked.

Marissa looked at her, and then, her eyes slid in my direction, which caused her daughter's to do the same.

"I know you," she said.

"Excuse me?" I replied, taken aback by the certainty of her statement.

"I know you. I mean, I've seen you somewhere before... What's your name?" she asked, looking at me curiously.

"Joy," I replied.

"As in Miss Joy? The photographer, right?" she asked, smiling and nodding.

I nodded too, relieved that she'd recognized me for my actual work and not my extracurricular activities. My relief was short lived though.

"I follow your work on social media, and your OnlyFans page is *lit*!" she said.

"Ava, what the fuck are you doing even knowing about OnlyFans?" Marissa asked.

I could see the look of terror in the older woman's eyes, but her daughter was facing me, so she was oblivious to the new secret that her mom had learned.

"Mom, try not to sound so old please. I'm nineteen, and I know what a dick and pussy is. They fit well when you put them together. Sorry not sorry. If you saw how Joy and her partner, Angelo, be getting down, then you'd probably subscribe too! Oh, my God though, the video from the plane, the one where you were playing the daddy/daughter roles, that shit was *hot!*" Ava said, coming to sit across from me in the spot that her mom had just vacated.

I was at a complete loss as to what I was supposed to say in this moment, but the longer that I stared at Ava, the more my curiosity grew. She definitely favored her mom, but some of her features reminded me of pictures I'd seen of Nate before he'd gotten a new face. When my eyes locked with Marissa's, I could almost feel her fear, which told me that the question on the tip of my tongue was one that she didn't want me to ask. I hesitated, but I couldn't stop the train of thought circling the tracks in my mind.

"I didn't know that Nate had an older daughter," I said, looking back at Ava.

"You know my dad?" she asked.

"Yeah, he's the one that sent me here because the nigga that I thought was my father is trying to kill me right now."

"That's why Nate sent you? Because of Ant?"

"Wait, Ant is your father? The same Ant that tried to kill us?" Ava asked, looking back at her mother.

"The very same," Marissa replied tightly.

"So, is that what was happening in the video that went viral on your Instagram the other day?" Ava asked, turning back to face me.

"What video?" Marissa asked.

"It's footage that was captured of an ambush where some hittas ran down on me in Chinatown in San Francisco, and I had to shake my way out," I replied.

"You killed someone?" Marissa asked.

"It was self-defense, Mom," Ava said defensively.

I could tell that Marissa was waiting on an answer to come from me, but my mouth remained shut from fear of incriminating myself.

"Listen, Joy, I'm not questioning you as a cop. I'm just trying to get a clear picture of what's going on," Marissa said, moving back to the couch and taking a seat beside her daughter.

I evaluated her cautiously for a moment, but then I realized that Nate wouldn't have set me up to go to prison, which meant that having Marissa for an ally was the only other alternative.

"Ant is trying to kill me because I moved all of his legal assets, and I refused to give them back. Niggas like him don't take kindly to being disobeyed, and the days of him playing dad are long gone," I confessed.

"Oh, wow... So, that video that you shot on the plane was real? Your partner could actually turn out to be your biological dad?" Ava asked in disbelief.

My eyes moved to Marissa, and her subtle shake of the head was all that I needed to see.

"Everyone in this world is connected somehow, but I'm more worried about staying alive at the moment," I replied, smoothly dogging the question.

"Where's Ant now?" Marissa asked.

"Still in federal holding in Petersburg, Virginia as far as I know. I went to see him a few days ago."

"I'm surprised that Nate didn't kill him when he and the chance," Marissa said, looking at me in search of an explanation.

"I don't think that it was designed to go like that because the CIA wanted him pretty bad, and they got him cold on a murder charge," I said.

"Who'd he kill?" Marissa asked.

I looked at Ava, noticing how raptly she was listening to this conversation, and I knew that now wasn't the time to reveal that her aunt was dead.

"I don't know who he killed. I just know that he's a killer, and I don't want anything to do with that," I replied.

"Speaking of killers, why is my dad helping you?" Ava asked curiously.

"Who knows why your dad does the shit that he does?" Marissa asked, attempting to spin Ava away from that line of questioning.

"Normally, I'd say that you're right, Mom, but this is the daughter of his sworn enemy, which means there has to be some type of angle he's exploiting," Ava replied.

"You don't think very highly of your father, do you?" I asked, feeling suddenly defensive of him.

"It's not about what I think. It's about what I know to be true based on experience. My dad will always choose strategy over emotion," Ava stated in a matter-of-fact tone.

"That's not necessarily true, sweetheart," Marissa said, locking eyes with me.

"Show me the proof," Ava challenged.

I couldn't explain the feelings inside me that made me want to defend the man that had turned my life upside down, but that was how I felt. Nate would never be perfect, but I knew from my own experience that he wasn't all bad.

"I'm the proof. Like you said, I was raised by his biggest rival, the man who murdered his mother, so if he was using strategy over emotion, then he wouldn't have sent me to a safe space. He would've just left me for dead."

"I mean, I could see why that would be true... but maybe you're worth more to him alive than you would be dead. Maybe he's playing the long game," Ava countered.

"There is no long game, Ava, because Ant is in CIA custody, and you know that your Uncle Stuckey ain't about to break that nigga out. It's over, and shit should be going back to normal sooner than later," Marissa predicted.

"Yeah, right," Ava replied cynically.

I knew that it wasn't my position to weigh in, so I just sat there quietly.

"Ava, stop assuming the worst about your father."

"Stop defending his bullshit all the time, Mom."

"You know, one day when you have kids, you'll realize that you're not a perfect person or a perfect parent, and then, you'll regret how you viewed your dad," Marissa insisted.

"At least your dad ain't trying to kill you," I mumbled.

Ava's eyes shifted toward mine, and I saw her empathy for me melt away some of the apathy she felt toward her father. She continued to stare at me for a few moments, and that was when I sensed a slight shift within her.

"The math ain't mathing. If my dad ain't using you in some way to get at Ant, then he's using you in another way. Based on your defense of him, I'd say that he's probably fucking you at the very least."

"Hold up, just because you subscribe to my OnlyFans page don't mean that you get to sit here and act like you know what I do with *my* pussy!" I replied heatedly.

"Don't get mad at me because you be on some ho shit, and that allows us regular muthafuckas to judge you," Ava replied, chuckling maliciously.

I could see Marissa shaking her head like she was trying to warn me not to take the bait, but it was too late for that shit. Ava needed to be checked real quick.

"You know what? You're right. I'm fucking your daddy, and I'm pregnant with his baby. Congrats, you're about to be a big sister, and now you know why he's protecting me. Do you feel better?"

# Chapter 7

(Nate)

I made the trip to D.C. in good time, and I went directly to Stuckey's safehouse. I could've went to my own spot in Maryland, but for what I had in mind, it was best that I leave no evidence of me ever being in this part of the country. Once I got into the apartment, I put in a call to one of my niggas, and then I took a quick shower to revive myself because I could feel the fatigue trying to overpower me.

When I finished that, I put on some of Stuckey's clothes and sat down in the living room to roll a blunt. I'd just put the finishing touches on the cherry flavored Backwood when I heard a knock at the front door, and I smiled inwardly, as I put flame to the end of my weed filled cigar. When I got up and opened the door, I found my nigga, Jackman, standing there with his bottom bitch, Kita, right next to him.

"Same old Jackman," I said, chuckling.

"You already know that I ain't bout to change my life for no one, my nigga. Now pass that blunt," he replied, smiling.

I obliged with the weed and stepped aside so that they could enter.

"Welcome back from the dead, Nate. I like your new face," Kita said, giving me a quick hug.

"You already know that I couldn't come back as no ugly nigga," I replied, laughing, as I closed the door and led them back into the living room.

As I sat down, I reflected on my relationship with this deadly couple. I'd crossed paths with Tez, aka Jackman, in a trap house in Alexandria, Virginia when I'd been at a dice game breaking niggas' pockets. He'd came in real calm and robbed that muthafucka blind with a Mossberg pump and a smile on his face the whole time. The nigga had worn no mask and showed no fear, which made him the perfect kind of stupid in my mind, but the part that I'd respected was that he'd came for the dope and dope money. He didn't rob the dice game, and every nigga that I knew would've definitely tried to rob us because there had been at least 30K on the ground.

After I'd witnessed that situation, I started doing some checking around on the nigga that everyone knew as Jackman. His reputation was one of murder, money, and mayhem, but the twist was Kita.

Kita was a 5'10", two hundred forty-pound chocolate man who'd made the transition into becoming a woman, and she made muthafuckas respect her as a bad bitch out in them streets. She'd captured the heart of Jackman, and he'd realigned both niggas and bitches' hairlines for playing with his Kita Boo. The thing about Jackman was that he was a 6'2", two hundred twenty-five-pound, light skin, pretty boy with a quick smile, so the average muthafuckas judged him without seeing beneath the surface.

Our first encounter after he'd robbed the trap house was at a local NA meeting where I sat and listened to addicts tell their stories of how drugs had ruined their lives. It had been my intent to ask him why he came to these meetings, but after the meeting was over, I found him posted up, discretely selling dope to some of the same addicts who "cherished" their sobriety. Lowkey, the nigga was making crazy money, and it wasn't an expected place to really move work, so I respected the genius of it. When there was a lull in his sales, I'd pulled up on him, and we'd had a brief conversation about his potential. The rest was history full of money, dead bodies, and calculated moves that formed a loyalty that allowed me to call on both of them now for assistance.

"So, what's up, my nigga? What's brought you back from the dead?" he asked, passing me my blunt back.

"That's a long story but just know that I need you to help me smoke at least two people," I replied before I hit the blunt.

"Who needs to die?" he asked without hesitation.

"The director and assistant director of the CIA," I said seriously.

Both Kita and Jackman looked at me for a moment without blinking, and then, they looked at each other.

"I think we're gonna need you to break down that long story real quick," Kita said.

Given what I was asking of them, I knew that this was a reasonable request, so I took it from the top and ran down a sanitized version of what had transpired in the past seven months. By the time I was done, the blunt was gone, but Jackman looked completely sober, and Kita was looking at me like I'd grown two heads.

"Damn, nigga, you've been busy. That shit that went down in Mexico was gruesome, which tells me that this nigga ain't bout to remember how to forget anytime soon. That means that your math is definitely mathing when it comes to him needing to die before you can stop looking over your shoulder. Tell me how Kita and I can help."

"It's simple really. I need access to the director and assistant director," I replied, smiling.

"Simple? Nigga, you might as well have said that you wanna smoke the president," Kita said, shaking her head.

I laughed because I knew that Kita was serious, albeit dramatic, with her response. We all knew that Kita was a queen in a city full of LBGTQ+ who knew the secrets of D.C.'s elite, and these secrets touched all branches of government. Most of the men involved were selling the illusion of being straight, especially with Donald Trump as president, and they were also married to women. In the end, what this meant was that favors could be used to draw my targets out into the open, and then I could add a date to their tombstone.

"What's the timeframe?" Jackman asked.

"The sooner I get to them, the sooner I can get to Ant," I replied.

The couple exchanged a look full of silent communication that left me somewhat curious, but instead of trying to solve this particular riddle, I got up and went into the kitchen. After retrieving a few beers, I returned to the living room, passing one to each of my guests, before taking my seat again. I could tell by the sour expression on Kita's face that something that Jackman had said didn't sit right with her.

"We'll help you, bruh," he said.

"Okay... but?" I asked, locking eyes with Kita.

"This ain't no ordinary request, know what I'm saying, so Kita feels like we should get paid, but you're family so..."

"I'll give you five million apiece tonight," I said, nonplussed by the money factor.

"Five-Five million?" Kita stammered, wearing a comical shocked expression on her face.

"I think that's fair, don't you?" I asked, looking from one to the other.

"That's more than enough, bruh," he replied, twisting the top off of his beer and taking a healthy swig.

I did the same and took a sip from my own beer before pulling out my phone and starting to pull the funds together. It took a quick ten minutes for me to move the money into the bank account that Jackman had provided, and the smile on his face said it all.

"Well, this can officially be our last job, and then we can retire somewhere tropical," he said.

"You mean it, baby?" Kita asked, grinning from ear to ear.

"You damn right. Shit, with this kind of money, we can go legit, go to a different country, and live like royalty," he replied seriously.

"Then let's get down to business," I said, feeling eager for a different type of fulfillment.

Kita pulled her phone out and called someone named Maxine, telling her to set a date with her most important client. When that was done, she called someone named Secret and told her the same thing.

"This shouldn't take long, but what do you want me to do once they arrive at their locations?" Kita asked.

"I want you to earn the five million that you just got. Send me photographic proof and make sure that their bodies drop in a semi-public place so that their secret double lives are exposed," I replied.

"We can do that. What's your plan though?" Jackman asked.

"Well, first, I gotta establish a very public alibi, and then, I'm gonna play the long game by waiting on my moment to attack Ant."

"Do you need anything else from us?" he asked.

"Not at the moment but be ready in case I've gotta improvise," I advised.

They both nodded and then drained the remnants of their beer before standing up. I followed their lead, accepting Jackman's hand extended my way, and then gave Kita a hug when she stepped forward.

"Be safe," I warned, looking at both of them seriously.

I could tell by the look in Jackman's eyes that he understood exactly how dangerous it was to kill two government agents, but he was raised in the same streets that had shown me that nobody was beyond the touch of death's grip. After I showed them to the door, I got to work on my alibi. I knew that I needed to have my time accounted for in case my name was ever suggested as a suspect, but that didn't mean that I needed a night out on the town for visibility purposes. I raided my brother's closet until I came out wearing a black, short sleeve button up with matching black slacks and a pair of black Tom Ford loafers. It would've been nice to have some arm candy, but I didn't need any more women to complicate my life with.

Once I left the house, it took twenty minutes before I pulled up outside of a jazz club named Angie's and passed the valet my keys. This used to be one of my favorite spots back in my single and mingling days, but I wasn't trolling for bad bitches tonight. I paid the cover charge in cash and then went in search of the owner. Big Angie was a Baltimore legend, and she'd moved more dope through the port than anyone since little Melvin. She stood 6'1", two hundred fifteen pounds of still fuckable ass and titties, with a chocolate mahogany skin tone. She had an easy smile for the people that she fucked with but hard eyes for all strangers. The latter was the look that I got when I found her sitting alone at her permanent table in the back.

"Still as beautiful as ever, I see."

"Nigga, do I know you?" she asked with open hostility.

"It's me, Nate."

"Nate who?"

"Stop playing, Ang. I changed my face, but my dick is still the same if you need me to pull it out," I said, smiling mischievously.

Her expression changed from one of hostility to one of curiosity, and I saw a challenge rise within her irises.

"You don't look like Nate, but you sound as cocky as the nigga I remember. It's gonna take more than some bold talk to convince me though," she replied, looking at my crotch and then up into my eyes.

I chuckled softly because I'd definitely walked myself into this predicament, but I wasn't ashamed of what I was working with, so I calmly unzipped my slacks and pulled my dick out. I heard a woman not far away from us gasp in surprise, but my attention was focused on Angie, whose eyes were locked on mine. She looked down at my dick for a few moments and then raised her glass in salute, as she sipped her liquor.

"The first time that you and I fucked was in the back storage room of this place, and I probably still have the scars from your nails on my back. Do you need a refresher course in good dick?"

"No, just put that muthafucka away before you cause a riot in this bitch and tell me what the fuck you want," she said, shaking her head and smiling.

I fixed my clothing so that I was once again concealed, and then I sat in the booth beside her. She signaled over one of the waiters and ordered me a double shot of Cognac, which told me that she really knew it was me behind this face.

"So, tell me, Nathan, what's brought you back from the dead because from what I'd heard, it was definitely safer for you to stay that way."

"Nothing and no one is safe as long as Ant is alive," I replied.

"And you think that you're gonna be the one to end his run? That boy has been like an unstoppable cockroach since he was young, and now he has the type of power that commands fear from everyone."

"Everyone except me," I said, looking at her so that she would know how serious I was.

"Yeah, you always were too stupid to be scared... What brings you here though because I'm not looking to get involved in the dick swinging contest between you and Ant. Even if it's not much of a competition," she said, smiling wryly.

"Don't worry, sweetheart. I'm not here to get you into anything. I just needed a spot to kill time."

"Meaning you need an alibi," she replied, nodding knowingly.

I didn't confirm or deny her suspicions. I just accepted the drink that the waiter brought me and sipped while tuning into the live band that was playing.

"You've done well with this place, Ang."

"Thanks. I'm completely legit now, and it feels good not to have to look over my shoulder for the IRS."

"Have you had to look over your shoulder for anyone else?"

My question caused her to look over at me for a brief second before she answered.

"Nathan, you of all people know that I can take care of myself. It's cute that you still worry about me though."

"You almost sound surprised, Ang. You know that you and I have enough history to fill several books, and if you ever need me, I'll be there."

"Why does it sound like you're about to ask for a favor?" she asked suspiciously.

I laughed out loud while shaking my head no.

"I'm really not about to put you in the middle of this shit, sweetheart, because this ain't your fight on no level, and you're too precious to be any type of collateral damage," I replied genuinely.

"Well, in that case, let's get drunk and see where the night takes us."

Her smile was mischievous and inviting all at the same time, causing me to laugh softly because I knew where she saw the night going. I'd never been able to resist her feminine charms whether drunk or sober, but that was before I'd gotten married. I didn't need the trouble that new pussy brought me, so I kept my eyes on the band and the conversation between her and I light enough to be innocent. It was almost a full two hours later when I felt my phone vibrating in my pocket, and I pulled it out to find a text message letting me know that Jackman and Kita had handled their business. I didn't doubt them, but the pictures of the two dead men were worth a thousand words. I immediately texted Stuckey and congratulated him on his job promotion, and I let him know that I'd be calling him from a secure phone sometime tomorrow.

"That smile on your face is pure evil, and it's enough to make a bitch's panties wet," Angie said, leaning over closely so that only I could hear her.

I chuckled, as I tossed back the rest of my drink and dug some money out of my pocket.

"I'm gonna have to take a raincheck on doing something with your delicious river, but I appreciate the time."

"Your money is no good here, but you make sure that you come back and see me," she said, pushing my hand away.

"I will," I promised, giving her a kiss on the check before sliding out of the booth and making my exit.

My mind was already working on the next phase of my plan now that I'd created a shake up in the CIA that would put my brother on top. I knew that right now, Stuckey was trying to see what angle I was playing, and he probably thought that I intended to use his new acquired position as interim director of the CIA to get to Ant. That wasn't the move though. The move was to get the CIA away from Ant so that I could use my other resources to get into a position to send him straight to hell. My plan was to make as many people as I could want Anthony dead, and that started by framing him for the murders of the CIA director and assistant director. It was an easy lie to sell, and as soon as I got back to my car, I was on my phone with my FBI connect, telling her my theory on the murders. Our conversation was brief, and when it ended, I sat there and contemplated what my next move should be.

Deep down, I knew what I had to do, even though I didn't wanna do it, so I started the car and headed for the airport. When I got to Regan National, I bought a one-way ticket to Colorado and waited an hour and fifteen minutes for the flight to board. I didn't bother to call ahead and tell anyone that I was coming because I still had no idea how this shit was gonna play out. All I knew was that it couldn't get any worse than what had happened with Tay... or at least I hoped that it didn't.

# Chapter 8

### (Joy)

The smile on Ava's face suddenly fell flat, as her eyes went to my stomach like she could miraculously see through me like an x-ray machine.

"You're lying," she said, sounding less self-assured and cocky.

"Am I? Well, you don't believe shit out of my mouth, so why don't you ask your dad? Better yet, just ask your mom," I suggested, smiling.

Marissa couldn't hide the look of distress covering her facial features and merging with her body language, so when Ava turned to look at her, she was like a deer in the headlights. Neither woman spoke, and a moment later, Ava turned back to face me head on.

"If you're really pregnant by my dad, then you're a dumber bitch than I thought you were."

I could tell by her comment that she hadn't made the connection between her dad and the man in all of my OnlyFans videos, but I decided to let that be a mystery solved later. I could feel Marissa's eyes on me, but I kept staring at Ava in case her emotions got the best of her common sense, and she needed me to fuck her up. I saw one of the security guys that had stopped me in the hallway enter the room out of my peripheral vision and go straight to Marissa. I couldn't hear what he was saying to her, but I saw her nod, and then, he turned to leave.

"Whatever happened between you and Nate is your business, so we don't gotta say no more about it," Marissa stated.

Her tone stated that what she was saying wasn't a suggestion. It was to be respected as the law. The look in Ava's eyes said that she wanted all the smoke, but she kept her mouth shut, and I didn't bait her. A few seconds later, an attractive, Black 6'1", two hundred forty-pound man entered the room and went straight to Marissa.

"What are you doing here?" she asked, opening her arms to hug him.

"Nate sent me."

His short response had my undivided attention, especially because I'd never seen him before. Ava turned around at the sound of his voice, and then, she got up and went around the couch toward him.

"Hey, Uncle Stuckey," she said, hugging him.

"Hey, sweetie. How are you holding up?" he asked.

"Going stir crazy for real, but Joy has brought enough drama to provide some new entertainment to relieve the monotony."

"Don't talk about me like I ain't right the fuck here," I said, feeling my irritation rise.

"I'm gonna need you to stop the bullshit for real," Marissa said, looking first to her daughter and then to me.

"So, I'm guessing that the awkward introductions have been made between you all. Hi, Joy, I'm Stuckey, Nate's brother and the peacemaker in this movie that is your life," he said, coming toward me, smiling with his hand extended.

I took his hand while analyzing the level of his sincerity and silently wondering where the fuck Nate was.

"Unc, where's my dad?" Ava asked, giving voice to my thoughts.

"He's handling some business," Stuckey replied evasively.

"Does this business have to do with Ant trying to kill Joy?" Marissa asked.

The questioning look that he gave me looked more than a little surprised that I'd divulged that much information to these women who were virtually strangers to me. They were obviously meant to be kept far removed from all the dirt that Nate was doing.

"Exactly how much did you say?" Stuckey asked softly, still looking at me.

"Not everything, trust me," I replied in the same tone, figuring that he was up to speed on everything involving me and his brother.

He gave me a curt nod and then turned back around to face Ava and Marissa.

"Honestly, I don't know what my brother is up to because he wanted me to have plausible deniability."

"That definitely sounds like he's up to no good," I said.

"Which is nothing new," Ava commented, shaking her head with an annoyed expression.

"Not too much on your dad though, Ava, because you know that he moves the world for those he loves," Stuckey said.

"Love? Who does he love? Me? My mom? This bitch?" Ava asked, nodding toward me.

I desperately wanted to take the bait and bump with my potential long-lost sister, but I kept shit cute and kept my mouth shut.

"Ava, calm down," Marissa said.

In response to that, Ava turned and left the room without speaking another word.

"Did Nate really think that *this* was a good idea?" I asked, gesturing toward myself and the surrounding environment.

"Believe me when I tell you that I asked him the same question, but I understand that his only concern was to make sure that you were out of harm's way," Stuckey replied.

"And then what? How does he plan to solve the problem that is Ant because it's obvious that whether that nigga is locked up or not, he's still dangerous on a lethal level," Marissa said.

"I'm starting to understand that now, despite Nate telling me that exact thing after Ant had been arrested. Once he's done with whatever he intends to do, I plan to go to the director of the CIA and have a serious conversation about Ant," Stuckey vowed.

"And what will that accomplish?" I asked curiously.

"I don't know, but Ant is a threat to national security, and that's something that the CIA is allowed to deal with through prosecution. I haven't checked with my sources inside the FBI to see if they have any plans for Ant, but that's my next move," Stuckey replied.

"What do we do in the meantime?" Marissa asked.

"Just continue to lay low, and in your case, you need to make sure that Ava and Joy don't kill each other," he replied, laughing softly.

"I'm glad this amuses you," I said sarcastically.

"I'm sorry. I'm not trying to laugh at your pain, but honestly, you're lucky to be alive after the shit you pulled with Nate's wife," Stuckey said.

"What's he talking about?" Marissa asked, directing her question to me.

"What I told you before about the video from the plane," I replied, unfazed by what Stuckey said.

"Damn, you told her that too?" he asked, sounding more than a little surprised.

"Yeah, I did. I mean, there's no point in her not knowing considering the fact that it was Nate who sent me out here. Obviously, she's someone that can be trusted," I replied, still staring at her.

"You're right, but please tell me that you didn't say all of this in front of Ava."

"No, not all of it. She's bound to do the math eventually though because she subscribes to my OnlyFans page, and once she sees Nate, she's sure to recognize his face."

Stuckey and Marissa shared a look. Before either of them could speak again, the sound of a phone ringing echoed throughout the room until Stuckey pulled it out and silenced it without looking at it.

"Why would you two make an OnlyFans page?" Marissa asked.

"It was Nate's idea, and I think it had to do with humiliating my parents."

The way that Stuckey was staring at me, I could tell that he was wondering if I'd spoken on the fact that Nate could be my father, but I gave him a subtle shake of the head. I saw the understanding in his eyes, along with relief, even though we both knew that the latter was temporary.

"I need to talk to my dumb ass baby daddy because…"

Marissa's words were interrupted by Stuckey's phone, but instead of a call, it was a factory set sound for incoming messages or notifications. I watched as he looked down, and whatever he read must've been serious because his eyes were suddenly bulging out of their sockets.

"What is it?" I asked.

He didn't reply, but when he looked back up at me, I could see both horror and confusion in his eyes.

"Stuckey... what is it?" Marissa asked, sounding genuinely concerned.

"The director and assistant director of the CIA have been murdered. Their bodies were found outside of a known gay club in D.C., and there were videos of both of them uploaded to Instagram that showed them getting head from two different trannies. They were fucking each other too."

"Oh, wow, that's crazy as fuck, not to mention nasty as a muthafucka," I said, shaking my head and wrinkling my nose up like I could smell the shit on a nigga's dick.

"The director and assistant director of the CIA?" Marissa asked, looking directly at Stuckey.

When his eyes shifted to hers, they were both silent, but this time, I was able to follow their train of thought.

"There are no coincidences and based on the look on both of your faces, I guess it's safe to assume that you both believe that Nate is somehow behind this," I said, looking from Marissa to Stuckey.

"That's exactly what I'm thinking, but why would he do that?" Marissa wondered aloud.

For a moment, nobody spoke, undoubtedly trying to figure out what angle Nate was playing. All I knew was that this nigga was certifiably crazy if he'd actually taken out the top of the CIA food chain. I was just about to ask Stuckey to call Nate so that I could talk to him when Stuckey's phone began ringing again, and he immediately answered.

The conversation lasted all of thirty seconds, and the only thing that Stuckey said was that he understood, and then he hung up.

"What's going on?" Marissa asked.

He didn't readily reply, but I could feel the tension radiating off of him in silent waves.

"That was the secretary of defense, and he told me that a meeting had just taken place in the war room at the White House," he replied.

"Sounds serious," I said.

"It is... What else did the secretary say?" Marissa asked curiously.

"Just that I'd been chosen as the interim director of the CIA, and my first official act was to coordinate with the FBI to find out who killed the former director and assistant director."

The gears in my mind shifted so fast, and this revelation illuminated what had been unseen, and I laughed out loud, which caused both Stuckey and Marissa to look at me.

"You okay?" Marissa asked.

"Yeah, I'm good, but I know that you see how crazy this is. I mean, obviously *this* was Nate's plan, and now, you're the head nigga in charge tasked with searching for a killer that your own brother sent," I replied.

"You're saying that Nate killed them in order to put Stuckey in charge? I don't know. That sounds farfetched, even for Nate's crazy ass," Marissa said skeptically.

"No, I think that Joy is right. This was definitely Nate's doing, and it explains why he kept me in the dark about everything. He knows that as the director, I can put Ant in a position where he's vulnerable enough to get killed."

"Are you gonna go through with it?" I asked, searching his face for a sign of what was next to come.

He looked at me for a moment before redirecting his attention back to his phone and making a call that he took into the next room.

"Is that what you want? For Nate to kill Ant?" Marissa asked.

"Honestly, I don't know. I just know that I don't want Ant to kill me and my baby, which means that someone has to stop him."

Her penetrating gaze evaluated me calmly, but I could tell that she was evaluating me to see where my loyalties were in this situation.

"You must be tired from your trip and the adventures prior to it, so why don't I show you to your room?" she offered, nodding toward the hallway that Ava had disappeared down. I didn't argue with her. I simply followed her down the hall until we came to a bedroom door. She opened it and stepped aside to allow me to enter. When I walked in, my eyes locked on the queen-sized bed in the middle of the room, and I crossed the soft carpet quickly to get to it. The only thing that I took off were my shoes, and then, I was sliding beneath the warm comforter. By the time my head hit the pillow, I could feel sleep pulling at me like the reaper was calling. If Marissa said something before she disappeared, I never heard it, and honestly, I didn't care at the moment. Right now, my body and my baby were demanding rest. I gave up the fight against sleep, and I was quickly transported into the realm of dreamland.

In my dreams, Nate and I were on some island, watching our beautiful, chunky baby girl playing in the sand not far away. It was so real that I could hear the crash of the waves and taste the sea salt in the air. When I suddenly woke up, I could feel tears sliding down my cheeks, and the sense of loss that I felt was causing my heart to hammer against my chest. When I pulled my phone out of my pocket, I saw that I'd only been sleep for a few hours, so I didn't understand what had woke me up until I heard a strange, muffled noise. At first, I didn't know what the noise was, but the repetition and cadence were familiar enough to pull me from beneath the warmth of the comforter. When I opened the door to the room that I was in, I was confronted by the pitch-black hallway, which caused me to use the light on my phone. I started to head in the direction of the living room, but that wasn't where the sound was coming from, so I headed in the opposite direction. Two doors down from mine was another bedroom with the door slightly ajar, and when I peeked in, I felt my mouth drop open and hit my chest. My instincts took over, and before I knew it, I was using my phone to record what I was seeing.

The passion that I saw on Marissa's face was the kind that couldn't be faked, which meant that the back shots Stuckey was feeding her were *definitely* good to her. Damn near made me wanna buy a ticket to ride that ride! The sheer concentration on his face told me that he wanted her to become a slave to his dick, and it was familiar because I'd seen the look on his brother's face when I'd watched the videos that him and I had made. As I continued to film the freak session, I wondered if Nate knew that his brother was fucking his baby mama. I made sure to zoom in on both of their faces, and I got lucky because Marissa picked that exact moment to cum hard enough to make her teeth rattle. I had to suppress my desire to give them both a round of applause before I backed away from the door and headed up the hallway toward the living room.

I desperately wanted to pour myself a drink to calm the lingering nerves that were still raw from my dream about Nathan and the family that we'd created. I was able to resist the urge, as I went in search of the kitchen, and once there, I poured myself a tall glass of milk. I'd downed half of it when I heard a commotion, which forced me to sit my glass on the counter and head back toward the living room. The sound of animated voices escalating was coming from the direction of the front door, and the first thing that I did was grab the Sig Sauer .45 with the rubber grip off of the coffee table before I went in that direction. When I looked out the peephole, my heart hit my toes, and the gun felt heavier against my palm, but none of that stopped me from pulling the door open.

"It's okay. Let him in," I said, locking eyes with Nate.

I saw his irritation swiftly evaporate, as he drank me in from head to toe, and I felt that familiar tingle in the pit of my stomach. I was silently cussing my own self out for being weak for this man, but outwardly, I kept my expression neutral, as I stepped aside to let him in. I closed the door and followed him into the living room, but once we got there, I was unsure of what to say or do.

"What are you doing here, Nate?"

"I came to check on you."

"That's cute. Now tell me the real reason that you're here," I said, not willing to fall for his smooth talk.

"Despite the stunt that you pulled with my wife, I still care about you and the baby that you're carrying. I wanted to see for myself that you were straight."

"Don't act too concerned, Nate, or I might think that you actually meant it when you said that you loved me," I replied somewhat sarcastically.

He didn't respond, but the look that he gave me moved my heart to my throat. The intensity of his stare was so hypnotic that I felt unable to pull my eyes away or move at all.

"Nate., what are you doing here?"

Without looking, I knew that question had come from Marissa, and I could hear the fear in her tone. Nate was still intently focused on me though, and I used that to save Marissa's life. For now.

"Come on, we need to talk in private," I said, nodding for him to follow me.

Thankfully, he fell into step with me and ignored Marissa, but once we got to my room, I didn't know what to say. I'd caged myself in with the lion, and now there was nowhere to go.

# Chapter 9

### (Nate)

I could tell that my physical presence was affecting everything in her, including her breathing because it was rattling like she'd ran ten miles to get to work. I suppressed the smile that came with this intimate understanding, and instead, I focused on her well-being.

"I know that I threw you out of the frying pan and into the fire with my baby mama and daughter. Tell me, how much did you tell them?" I asked curiously.

"Marissa knows damn near everything, but the bigger problem is that Ava subscribes to our OnlyFans page."

I did the mental math rapidly, and what it added up to left me feeling more than a little distressed.

"So, you're telling me that she knows about you being... about the possibility of you being my daughter?" I asked, speaking softly but looking at her with explosive heat.

I knew that now wasn't the time to point out that I was the one to insist that there was *no* possibility of her being my daughter, so I kept my focus on the issue.

"All I'm saying is that when Ava sees your face, she's gonna recognize you and do the math, which means she's gonna tell her mom," she replied logically.

I started to point out the fact that we were consenting adults, but that wasn't any type of point that I could stand on with Ava, and I knew it. That only left me with one option.

"We need to leave while she's still asleep," I said.

"We? I thought that you sent me here to keep me safe."

"I did, but that was before I knew that our sex life was about to be discovered by two females that I know can be *more than* volatile. Right now, the safest place for you is with me, so let's go," I said.

She stood still for a few moments, staring at me while debating something within the waves of her mind. I knew and understood that she didn't trust me, but this wasn't about that right now. All that mattered was keeping her and our baby safe with as little stress as possible.

"Where are we going?" she asked.

"Honestly, I don't know, but I figure that out of the country is a safe first move."

"Especially with you shaking up the food chain at the CIA?" she asked, giving me a purposely blank look.

I didn't look away or answer the question, which signaled that this line of conversation was over. Before she could press the issue, there was a knock on the bedroom door that distracted us.

"Yeah?" she called out.

When I looked over her shoulder, I saw the door open, and Stuckey's eyes locked with mine.

What's-What's up, bruh?" he asked, sounding weird.

"Nothing. You ready to be the head nigga in charge?" I asked, switching the topic away from what he'd walked in on.

"I got your congratulations text, but I don't like this crazy ass scheme that you've put together. As badly as I know that Ant needs to die, I can't be the one to orchestrate that," he replied sincerely.

"I don't need you to do anything other than follow the breadcrumbs," I said.

"And what *exactly* does that mean?" he asked, narrowing his gaze on my face.

"That means that without a doubt, the CIA is gonna thoroughly investigate the murder of your brethren, and when you look, you'll find that Ant is behind the assassinations," I replied smugly.

"Do I even wanna know how you managed to do that?" he asked, sighing deeply with exasperation.

I shook my head no and left that part of the conversation alone.

"Okay, so what's your next move?" he asked finally.

"It's still better if you don't know, but it's still a good idea for you to be here looking after Marissa and Ava. You know that I love Marissa, but Ava can be more than a little defiant and hard to handle, so having a presence that she'll respect will help a lot. Don't worry, I'll explain shit to Marissa so that she doesn't cuss you out for hovering," I assured him.

An unexpected chuckle that came from Joy caused all eyes to turn in her direction, but she quickly gathered her composure.

"What about her?" he asked, nodding toward Joy.

"I'm taking her with me."

"Do you think that's best?" he asked, giving me a knowing look.

"I think that it's a necessary move, but whether it's not my best move remains to be seen. What I do know is that if she stays here then shit is gonna get ugly."

He nodded his understanding, and when he looked back toward Joy, some type of message passed between them. I didn't give it much analytical thought because my mind was full of possible destinations we could hide out in.

"Grab your stuff so that we can go. I've got a rental car downstairs," I said.

"I've got one bag, and we don't need your rental because I bought a new car that's untraceable."

When I looked at her curiously, I was immediately reminded of how capable she was, and that was sexy as fuck.

"I'll drive," I said, holding my hand out toward her.

She passed me the keys without argument, and I turned back to my brother.

"Make sure that Ava don't know I was here. Where's Marissa?"

"She's-uh-in the shower, I think, but I'll let her know that you had to go," he replied.

"Say less. Let's go," I said, taking Joy's hand and leading her out of the room past Stuckey.

I'd halfway expected her to pull away from me, but our hands fit as comfortably as when we'd been a fake real couple. We strolled past Marissa's security detail without being stopped or questioned, despite the pretty pistol that Joy was still clutching. She didn't tuck it under her shirt until we reached the lobby, and then we made it to her car without incident.

"You definitely got good taste," I said, admiring the Porsche 911 turbo.

"At least when it comes to cars."

Her smartass reply made me chuckle, even though I knew it was directed straight at me, as I let her hand go and slid behind the wheel. Once she climbed in next to me, I fired up the engine and left a cloud of dust to go along with the smell of burnt rubber.

"Drive it like you stole it then," she said.

That was exactly my intent, but first, I had to decide where we were going. As soon as I saw the exits for the highway, I knew just where to go that was beyond Ant's reach, and it would most likely be the last place that he thought to look. I pulled my phone out, dialed a number, and listened to it ring five times before it was answered.

"Oscar, it's me. I'm on my way to you, and I need a place for me and a friend to lay low."

I listened to him cuss me out in Spanish for waking me up, but then, he gave me an address and hung up.

"Where are we going?" Joy asked.

"Mexico."

"Mexico? I didn't pack my passport, so how do you expect me to get across the border?" she asked.

"You really expect me to believe that you went on the run without a passport on you?" I asked, looking over at her, as I shifted gears fast to demand more speed from the car.

"I don't care what you believe, but what I'm telling you is that I'm not 'bout to have my passport stamped showing that I entered Mexico."

The way that she explained her defiance made sense to me, and I immediately pulled my phone back up and texted Oscar so that he could get us across the border discretely. I let him know what kind of car we were rolling in, and a few minutes later, he told me that he would take care of it.

"We should be okay to cross the border with ID," I said.

"And then what?"

"Well, and then we get some sleep and figure out what to do next," I replied.

"I don't understand why you don't just have your brother take Ant out now that he's at the top of the CIA."

"Because that would be too obvious and easy to link him to me. Don't worry though because the FBI will take care of Ant," I replied.

"The FBI? What the fuck do they have to do with anything?" she asked, confused.

"The FBI are like the watchers of the watchers. The CIA mostly operates in different countries around the world, and the FBI deals with domestic issues. Being that this was two government agents who were murdered, I pulled some strings to make sure the FBI is involved."

"And that's what you want?" she asked.

I nodded while keeping my eyes on the road. We rode in silence for damn near an hour, and I thought that she simply fell asleep until she spoke.

"I'm sorry, Nate."

"For what?" I asked, confused by her apology.

"For sending that to your wife... At the time, I felt validated because of everything that you had done and all that you'd put me through, but in the end, I hurt an innocent woman. She didn't deserve that, and neither did you."

"Actually, I did deserve it, and so much more for the ways that I hurt you. So, I accept your apology, but I want you to know that I'm sorry too," I said, looking over at her.

Even in the shadows, I could see her surprise, and the silence that settled between us wasn't awkward or uncomfortable. After a while, she readjusted in her seat and took my hand in hers. When I looked over at her, I saw that her eyes were closed, and she was headed for sleep. I didn't pull my hand away, but I didn't let it interrupt my thoughts of Ant's imminent demise. Knowing that this nigga had more lives than any cat, I knew that I needed to keep my mind focused on the plan for after he became America's most wanted. I drove through the night and into the sunrise, and by morning, I'd made a brief stop at the border before I was waved through by the Mexican federales. From that point, I received an armed escort to a house on the outskirts of Tijuana.

"Joy," I said, squeezing her hand gently.

Her eyes opened slowly, and the smile that she gave me was reminiscent of our mornings together in San Francisco, which seemed like a lifetime ago.

"I'm hungry," she said, stretching in a way that had my eyes fixated on her flexible body.

"I got you. Come on," I replied, stepping out of the car and heading toward the front door.

By the time we reached the first step, the front door opened, and a small Spanish woman stood there, cradling a shotgun like it was a newborn.

"Oscar sent me," I said, holding my hands up to show that I wasn't armed, and I posed no threat.

She stared at both of us for a few seconds, and then she stepped aside to allow us to enter. I reached for Joy's hand, and she was right there with me, as we walked up the steps and short patch of dirt to reach the front door. Once we were inside, the woman put the shotgun down and turned to us.

"My name is Marcia. Oscar told me to look after you, and he'd be here sometime later today. There's a room at the end of the hallway for you two, and I'll bring you some food when I'm done cooking," she said, pointing in the direction we were supposed to go in.

"Gracias," I replied, still holding onto Joy's hand, as I led the way up the hall to the bedroom that was camouflaged and hidden within the wall.

When I pushed the door open wider, I actually felt like I'd stepped into a third world country because all that was in the tiny room was a twin bed and four walls that were desperately depending on each other not to collapse.

"Couldn't we have just stayed at a motel?" Joy asked.

"The goal is to stay completely off of the radar, but this is only temporary because we're just passing through. The plan is for us to get some sleep and then head farther into South America before we jump to another continent," I explained, looking over at her.

The skepticism and uncomfortable feelings were obvious on her face, but I knew exactly how to distract her. After pulling her all the way inside the room, I shut the door and pulled her soft body right up against mine.

"Wh-What are you doing?" she asked, seemingly startled.

"Making the most of our time together," I replied, kissing her neck softly.

I felt her body tense up in preparation to resist whatever feelings I was causing inside her, but as soon as I touched my lips to hers, I felt all of her resistance evaporate. Our kiss was long and deep, and it caused our hands to attack our clothing that was separating our quickly heating flesh.

Once we were naked, I scooped her up and laid her down on the bed, pleasantly surprised by how soft it was, and I climbed on top of her like she was my favorite ride at the amusement park.

"Nate, we shouldn't," she whispered in between kisses.

"I know," I replied, sliding in between her swiftly opening legs.

"Ohhh, shit," she moaned, as I drove my dick inside her with enough force to disrupt her breathing.

I felt my lungs constrict while I adjusted to the pressure of her pussy's grip, but it wasn't long before I found my sea legs, and I was able to navigate her vast ocean. Despite our complicated history, I was determined to fuck her like she was a complete stranger. With this thought in mind, I threw both of her legs over my shoulders, and I folded her little ass up while I gave her drilling strokes that left her grunting my name. I fucked her like that for a solid ten minutes, and I was rewarded with her pussy drenching me from the waves of her first orgasm.

While she was still trying to catch her breath, I turned her on her side, separating us for a couple seconds, and then I was back inside her walls like a prisoner known for bad behavior. My fingers found her clit, and I spoke to her like someone reading braille while long stroking her with this good dick.

"No, Nate, don't," she begged, putting her hand on top of mine.

I let my actions speak for me, as I waited for that storm inside her to reach its peak. When I knew that she couldn't protect herself from sinking like the Titanic, I increased my speed and pounded us both into the blinding light of orgasmic fulfillment. With the amount of cum that I pumped into her, I knew that if she hadn't already been pregnant, then nine months from now, we'd definitely have a twin running around. When I finally pulled out of her, I laid down beside her and pulled her into my arms. She came willingly enough, and then, all I heard was her breathing deeply.

After a while, I drifted off into a dreamless sleep with her, finally giving in to the exhaustion that had been stalking me since North Carolina. I didn't know how long I slept, but when I opened my eyes, Joy was still in my embrace, clutching my arms that were wrapped around her. I could feel myself smiling, as I drifted back off, and when I opened my eyes again, the sun was making its slow rise above the hills in the distance. My body felt stiff from laying in the same position all night long, and I knew Joy had to be experiencing the same thing because she hadn't moved. I kissed her neck softly before unwrapping myself from around her carefully. I was just about to get out of bed when I heard the sounds of a phone chiming, and I knew that it wasn't mine. My curiosity got the best of me, causing me to get up and reach inside of her jeans pocket and extract her phone with the delicacy of a diamond thief.

The chiming had been an incoming text message, and the only thing that it said was that there was nowhere she could run or hide because she was already dead. There was no name on it but given everything that I knew, it was easy to deduce that this was Ant's work of intimidation.

I decided to check her messages to see how many she'd gotten like the one I'd just read, but before I could get too deep into her history, I came upon a video that froze me. The sight of Marissa's face in the throes of passion confused me at first, but once I pressed play, I understood exactly what the fuck I was seeing. The blood in my veins felt hotter than volcanic lava, but I managed to keep from screaming the rage that betrayal had put in my throat. I knew that I didn't have any right to dictate Marissa's life. It was just some foul shit for her and my own brother to be fucking. I suddenly wanted nothing more than to destroy them both, but that would have to wait. I slid her phone in my pocket, as I headed for the bedroom door, already contemplating what my rage would look like, but as soon as I opened the door, my mind shifted into battle mode.

The smell wafting on the air was a familiar one, as familiar as the taste of pussy on my tongue. It was blood. I closed the door softly and went in search of the pistol Joy had on her when we came in. After locating it in the pile of clothes, I quickly shook her awake while keeping my hand over her mouth to keep her from crying out.

"We gotta go. Somebody's been here, and they brought death with them."

# Chapter 10

(Joy)

The panic coursing through my body pulled me from the grogginess of sleep to full Pentagon alert status like a terrorist attack was imminent. The look in Nate's eyes wasn't one of panic, but it was so sincere that there was no question that we were somehow in danger. I scrambled up from the tiny mattress and got dressed fast enough to impress Clark Kent.

"Where's my gun?" I whispered, looking around the room frantically like a child missing a pacifier.

He held up the pistol in his hand while putting a finger to his lips and motioning for me to come to him. I closed the short distance between us and stood behind him, as he slowly pulled the door open. I couldn't hear a damn thing, so I had no idea what he was basing his information on, but I trusted him enough to stay right on his heels, as he crept up the hallway with the Sig Sauer out in front of him. I could feel the energy in his body was ready to knock a nigga's head off.

When we made it to the living room area, it looked the same as it had when we arrived, but there was a weight that I felt on my shoulders like a menacing presence. I'd expected Nate to head for the front door, but instead, he made a right turn and led us down another short hallway to the kitchen. As soon as we walked in, I was hit by the overpowering smell of blood, which caused my stomach to lurch violently in protest, but when I saw the severed head of the woman who'd let us in just sitting on the kitchen counter, I doubled over and vomited.

I'd witnessed death and brought it on someone in self-defense, but this was so much worse. Whoever had killed Marcia had strategically positioned her head in between a jar of peanut butter on the right and a jar of grape jelly to the left. The expression of horror on her face gave the whole scene a haunted house feeling, and I just wanted to get the fuck outta here.

"N-Nate, we need to leave," I whispered, pulling on his arm.

He didn't argue or resist, and he shielded my view from whatever other horrors the kitchen had to offer, as he gently pushed me backwards into the hallway. He took my hand in his, and we quickly made our way to the front room. The sun had risen, but I could tell that it was still early because when he opened the front door and we stepped outside, there was no one around. Only a stray cat roamed the streets.

"Get in," he said, nodding toward my car, as he went to the driver's side with the gun in his hand still up and ready.

We both managed to get inside without any shots ringing out, but it wasn't until we were on the move that I felt comfortable enough to speak.

"Who did that to her?" I asked.

"I don't know, but my guess is someone who was paid to do it."

"Do you think it has anything to do with us?" I asked.

"I'd say that's a safe bet," he replied, chuckling without humor.

I studied his profile for a moment, and I immediately got the sense that there was some shit that he wasn't telling me.

"What am I missing?"

His response was to dig in his pocket in between his rapid gear shifting and toss me my phone.

"Check your texts," he said.

It was on the tip of my tongue to ask how the fuck he got my phone, but that would be a conversation for later. I went to my messages, and as soon as I read the threat, I knew exactly who was responsible for that poor woman losing her head back there.

"Ant," I said, shaking my head in disgust.

"Yep, it would seem that daddy dearest really ain't giving up on the idea of your premature demise. That don't surprise me though because he don't know how to forgive or forget. Neither do I."

"So, what's your plan?" I asked, already noticing that he was retracing our route back to the border.

"Well, for starters, we're getting the fuck out of Mexico because either my nigga, Oscar, is no longer alive or he's no longer in control of the situation out here. I don't know who Marcia was to him, but he was the one who sent us there, and now she's dead. So, we're not safe here. Once we get back across, I'll figure out our next move."

"Wouldn't it be safer to head back to Colorado considering that your baby mama has her own private government army guarding her location?" I asked.

"She's also fucking my brother... Or did you forget what you recorded on your phone?" he asked, glancing over at me.

I could feel my mouth hanging open, but there was nothing I could say. We rode in silence, and the next thing I knew, we were back at the U.S./Mexico border. I held my breath until we made it through the checkpoint, and then I tried to figure out what to say to Nate.

"I didn't know if you knew what was going on between them, and I knew that you wouldn't believe me without proof, so I..."

"I get it," he replied shortly.

I knew that he wasn't the type to vent his feelings of betrayal, but I could feel his pain and anger radiating off of him like rays from the sun that was getting higher in the sky. Despite everything he'd taken me through, I still felt bad for him, but the only way that I felt safe expressing that was to put my hand on top of his. He didn't shake me off, even though it took a few minutes for him to interlock our fingers together.

"Where are we going?" I asked.

"I need to get you somewhere safe."

"I'm safe with you," I stated confidently, still surprising myself with the conviction that I felt when I said that.

"I know that you are, but I gotta kill Ant, and I don't want you there when that happens."

"I get that... But where can I go for real? The nigga just tracked us to what was supposed to be a safehouse in Mexico, and he obviously wants me dead more than you right now, so I don't know that us separating is the best move," I replied.

When he looked over at me, I saw understanding in his eyes, just below the iron will of determination.

"I've got a few friends that will provide assistance, but if you're gonna be with me on this, then you gotta do what I tell you when I tell you. Agreed?"

"Sounds kinky but I got you," I replied, smiling at him.

He nodded with a slight smile pulling at the corners of his mouth, and we rode on in silence. We didn't stop for a break to stretch our legs until we reached the Texas/Arizona state line. At a rest stop, Nate told me to get us some snacks and use the bathroom, while he made a call and refueled the car. I wasted no time because our baby was pushing on my bladder something vicious, and by the time I was squatting over the dingy toilet seat, I was pissing with the pressure of a busted fire hydrant. After relieving myself and washing my hands, I pulled my phone out to see if I had any new text messages. I found none but seeing that video sitting there made me feel differently than when I'd actually recorded it because now I knew that both people involved had hurt Nate. In my own twisted logic, this was unacceptable. I could do what I wanted to do to Nate, but God help the next muthafucka who tried that!

With this thought in mind, I pulled the video up and posted that bitch everywhere, beginning with the official CIA website since Stuckey was now the acting director. Knowing that this was scandalous and oh so salacious, I smiled, as I made sure to tag all of Marissa's associates in D.C. since she was still the chief of police. When I was done, I exited the bathroom, went to grab the food, and went back to the car where I found Nate waiting on me.

"Why do you have that shit eating grin on your face?" he asked, studying me thoroughly.

"No reason. So, where are we headed to?"

"There's good news and bad news on that front. I spoke to my FBI contact, and the good news is that they just charged Ant with two counts of capital murder, and they're planning to have him sent to a black site prison that's off the grid. He won't be able to contact anyone. The bad news is that they found out that he put a five-million-dollar bounty on my head and a twenty-million-dollar bounty on your head," he said, taking two bags of BBQ chips and a cupcake from my collection.

"That's a lot of money... which means muthafuckas ain't gonna wait to hear our side of the story he's spinning."

"My thoughts exactly, which explains why someone was bold enough to make their move in Mexico," he said, nodding his head.

"Okay, so what's your plan now?" I asked, looking at him closely.

"Well, my people in the FBI have offered us protection, and they've taken the APB off of your back for what happened in San Francisco. It's obvious to them now that you were acting in self-defense."

"That's good... But you don't sound too convinced about being protected by the Feds. So, what's the real plan?" I asked.

"To find out where the black site prison is and erase it like it never existed. Cut off the head and the body will sure enough fall."

What he said made sense, but the unspoken danger was what I was thinking about.

"Okay, so where do we go while you wait on this location to be revealed?" I asked.

"Underground," he replied, nodding for me to get in the car.

He followed my lead, but before I let him pull off, I turned in my seat to face him.

"In the interest of full disclosure, I need to tell you what I did."

"The fuck you do now?" he asked, sounding a little more than exasperated.

"Calm down, it ain't that bad. I just put up the video of your brother and baby mama."

"You what? Why would you do that?" he asked, sounding somewhat calmer.

"Because I don't like the way they both tried to play in your fucking face, so I put they trifling ass on blast. Period," I replied sincerely.

He stared at me for a moment before starting the car and pulling off. The silence seemed to be getting heavier by the second until he surprised the shit out of me when he burst into spontaneous laughter.

"You good?" I asked.

"Yeah, your ass is just crazy and bipolar as a muthafucka."

"Thank you, baby. As long as you know that then you know not to play with me again," I replied, smiling sweetly.

"Fair enough."

When he reached for my hand, I gave it to him with ease, and we rode like that until we pulled up at a little motel in Arizona. He got out and went to get us a room, and while he did that, I checked my phone to see what the reaction was to

Stuckey and Marissa. Of course, it had gone viral with the hashtags #governmentfunding and #interofficecooperation. I laughed at it while shaking my head, but my smile dried up quick when I saw a familiar face in my DMs with a message attached. In my quest to find out exactly who the fuck I'd let get me pregnant, I'd found pictures of him with his old face and pictures of his wife too, which was why I recognized her now. Her message was very simple and direct because all she wanted to know was if her husband was with me. I started to respond with some smart shit about us having to share him now for life, but I didn't need to antagonize her or piss him off. Plus, I needed him with a clear head. I was debating on whether or not to even tell him about it until he slid back into the seat beside me.

"You got a problem," I said, passing him my phone.

He looked at it for a few moments before passing it back to me.

"Ignore her."

"Why would she come to me though?" I asked curiously.

"I don't know, but I'm not in the mood for a crash out argument right now, so just leave her on read," he insisted, starting the car and driving us around the corner to our room.

When I got out of the car, I made sure to bring my bag so that I could take a much-needed shower and change clothes.

"If you need me, I'll be in the bathroom," I said, heading in that direction.

"Okay, I'mma order us some real food. Do you have any preferences?"

I thought about it, and that was when I understood what this 'baby brain' was that different women had described on Facebook and Instagram.

"I want a thick steak, cooked medium rare, with some butter pecan ice cream on the side, and some King's Hawaiian rolls. Oh, and don't forget the sweet tea. Make sure you get some steak and cheese egg rolls too," I said, already licking my lips in anticipation.

He laughed out loud, but he was smart enough to keep his mouth shut, as he headed back out the door. I went into the bathroom, thankful that it was so clean, and ran me a nice hot bubble bath. While the tub filled, I stripped down and put my phone on the tub's edge so that I could scroll on social media while I relaxed. I'd just gotten comfortable within the soothing bubbles with my phone in hand when another DM came through from Nate's wife. My intent was to ignore it, but it came with a video attached, and my curiosity got the best of me. When I watched the video, I felt my mouth drop open wide enough to make me believe that I was seconds away from tasting bubbles. I immediately messaged her back and asked her if the video was real and, if so, how the fuck was it possible.

It took her a few minutes, but eventually, she gave me enough of the story for shit to make sense. When I asked her what she intended to do, she gave me the simple reply that she needed Nate. Her earlier message made sense now, but with the current drama she'd just spilled to me, I was even more certain that it wasn't the time to be messy by admitting that he was with me. So, instead, I sent her a message back saying that I would contact Nate's other baby mama and ask her if she knew exactly where he was. I didn't mind putting the petty shit aside for the sake of what was now my extended family of sorts, and I knew that the last thing that Nate's wife needed was the image of him and I laid up in a motel room.

She didn't message me back, so I finished soaking in the tub until my body felt relaxed, and then, I washed up so that I could get out. By the time I was wrapping the Terry cloth robe around my naked body, I could hear Nate coming back into the motel room, and I hurried out to meet him.

"There's a big problem with your son, and your wife messaged me again."

His actions of taking the food out of various bags and putting it on the table froze, and his eyes came up to meet mine.

"What's wrong with my son?" he asked in a deadly whisper.

"He was detained by ICE agents because they're trying to say that he doesn't have legal citizenship status. I don't understand though because he's still a baby, and he was born here."

Nate was standing so still that I almost thought that he hadn't heard me until he started shaking his head.

"He was conceived state side, but we were out of the country on vacation when he was born," he said.

"Okay, but both of his parents are U.S. citizens, so doesn't that give him some type of immunity?"

"It used to, but President Trump fucked up immigration laws within his first one hundred days of his second presidential term. It's not safe for minorities that were actually born and raised here, so ain't no way in hell that *anyone* born in a foreign country is safe," he replied, visibly getting more agitated.

"Who would report a baby to ICE though?" I asked, still trying to understand the purpose of this move.

"Honestly, I don't know. It's easy to blame Ant, but what does he gain by getting my son deported to Paris, France?"

"It could be a scare tactic to force me back into the country so that our child will be born in the United States. Or..."

"Or what?" he asked, looking at me intently.

"Or Ant did it because he knows you'll go to France to get your son, meaning he'll know exactly where to find you."

I watched him contemplate my words, first with a look of doubt and then with one of understanding.

"He's splitting my focus, hoping to leave you vulnerable while I focus on the chaos he's created with my son, which means that I've gotta make sure you're safe before I go back to North Carolina," he said.

"Keep me safe where?"

I knew the answer to this question even before he opened his mouth, and I was already regretting my decision to set that particular bridge on fire.

"Come and eat because we're leaving after we get a few hours of sleep," he instructed.

I wanted to argue, but there was no time for that because this was bigger than all of us. Ant had involved an innocent child, and I knew that meant the gloves were coming off as far as Nate was concerned. He was bringing hell's fire.

# Chapter 11

(Nate)
(One Day Later-Colorado)

"Okay, listen up because I'm only gonna say this shit once," I stated, looking around the room and locking eyes with Stuckey, Marissa, Ava, and Joy.

When I was sure that I had everyone's undivided attention, I continued.

"I don't give a fuck what issues you all have with each other because the shit that's going on is deeper than that. Before I leave, we're gonna put all of this shit on the table because I don't want you fighting amongst each other while I'm gone. So, who wants to speak first?"

"Nate, I'm sorry about me and Stuckey. We never meant…"

"Save all that shit because I really ain't trying to hear it. What's next?" I asked.

"Is she really pregnant by you?" Ava asked, nodding toward Joy.

"Yeah," I replied shortly.

"Are you planning to get a DNA test?" Ava asked.

"DNA test for what? I ain't no bop ass bitch who don't know who she's pregnant by," Joy stated heatedly.

"I was talking about a DNA test between you and him to find out if he's actually your father," Ava said, wrinkling her nose up to show her distaste at the very idea.

"We ain't gotta do that because I know that her mom was lying," I replied.

"You mean you *hope* that her mom was lying," Stuckey said.

The look that I levelled at that nigga told him that his best move was to shut the fuck up because he was definitely lucky that I hadn't shot his ass yet.

"Are there any other issues that you all wanna address?" I asked, looking around.

"I'm glad that it's not important to you whether or not you're fucking your own biological daughter, but you're obviously judging my mom and Uncle Stuckey for hooking up," Ava said sarcastically, crossing her arms over her chest.

I opened my mouth to speak, but Joy was quicker.

"Sounds like you jealous, sis. Do you want some of Daddy's good dick?" Joy asked, smiling devilishly.

"Ewww, you're so fucking disgusting!" Ava said angrily.

"You didn't think that when you were watching us on OnlyFans. You was probably playing with that little pussy between your legs, and now you're throwing your guilt off on me," Joy taunted.

"Enough, both of you. I'm not 'bout to hear this bickering bullshit between you while you're forced to be around each other. Ava, stay on this side of the penthouse, and Joy, you stay on the other," Marissa said, pointing to emphasize her meaning.

I appreciated her taking control, but it still sickened me to look at her or my brother.

"Come on, Joy. Let's get you settled," I said, standing up and grabbing the one bag that contained all her worldly possessions.

She got up and followed me across the room and down a hallway that was identical to the other side of the penthouse's suite. I made a left into the first bedroom and set her bag on the end of the bed.

"You sure that I'm gonna be safe here?" she asked.

"Yeah, because I know that you can hold your own. Just stand your ground and don't show fear because if you do that, they'll attack like rabid dogs."

"Sounds more like a pack of hyenas," she replied, crossing the room to stand in front of me.

I chuckled lightly because there was definitely truth in her statement.

"You'll be fine. Just remember that you're carrying our child and try to keep your stress levels down."

"I need *you* to remember that I'm carrying our child and make sure that you come back safely to us. I know how Important it is for you to get your son back, but your new son or daughter is gonna need you just as much. Understand?"

I nodded and then placed a kiss on her forehead before I stepped around her and went back to the living room.

"Stuckey, let's go," I said.

"Hold up, Nate. Let me holla at you," Marissa said, standing up and coming toward me.

Apparently, she could see the resistance in my demeanor because it took her pulling me by the arm to get me to follow her out onto the balcony.

"What do you want, Marissa?"

"I want you to forgive me for having a moment of weakness. I swear to you on Ava's life that Stuckey and I had never had sex before that night. We'd never fucked around at all. Yeah, we've flirted harmlessly over the years, but we knew not to cross that line. What you saw was a whole bottle of 1800 tequila," she explained.

"Are you seriously blaming it on the alcohol?"

"I *know* how it sounds, but that don't make it any less true. I don't have real feelings for your brother. We all just have history in common," she said.

"Yeah, whatever. I got shit to do," I replied, leaving her on the balcony, as I walked back inside, headed for the front door.

Stuckey fell into step behind me, and the nigga was smart enough to keep his mouth shut until we were in Joy's car on the move.

"What's the plan?" he asked.

"For you to use your government credentials and connections to get my son out of the custody of the French authorities."

"Okay, and then what? I can't just bring him back into the States because ICE could pull the same move."

"I'll meet you in Madrid, Spain in two days to get him from you, so all you have to do is sit tight," I replied.

"Okay. What else do you need?"

"I need to know where the black site prison is that Ant got moved to," I replied, glancing over at him while shifting gears rapidly.

I could feel his hesitation because it was as palpable as the tension between him and I, but he knew that he was gonna tell me what I wanted to know.

"It's in Louisiana, right outside of Shreveport," he replied, pulling his phone out.

A few moments later, my phone vibrated, and I assumed that he'd texted me the exact location. We rode the rest of the way in awkward silence until we arrived at the airport and parked in the long-term lot.

"Where are you going?" he asked.

"Home to console my wife. Text me when you have my son, and I'll catch the next flight out. I'll send you the address where to meet me in Spain," I replied.

He nodded, and we both got out of the car to head for the terminal. Once we'd gone our separate ways, I went to the American Airlines window and bought a one-way ticket on the next red eye flight to North Carolina. I was set to depart in less than half an hour, and I would arrive in Charlotte within three hours, so I texted Tay and told her what time to pick me up from the airport. While I waited on them to do the boarding call for my flight, I tried to organize the noise in my mind so that I could plan my next move. I had faith that Stuckey could get my son back just by waving his CIA credentials because France didn't like international incidents, which meant that I could focus solely on Ant. I knew that getting to him inside of a black site prison was damn near mission impossible, and even if I could figure out a way in, it would take too long because the bounties that Ant had put on us were real and motivating to those niggas starving in the streets. This knowledge left me with nothing but drastic measures to take. I sent a message to Jackman requesting his services again, and within a few minutes, I got a message back, stating that what I wanted would cost no less than $25 million. I transferred $30 million to his account and told him that this was a high priority rush order. I got a thumbs up emoji a few seconds later, followed by the call for my flight to now board. I quickly made my way onto the plane and ordered two shots of Branson Cognac on the way to my seat. After my liquor was delivered and consumed, I texted Joy to let her know what was going on and to make sure that she was okay.

Her response was that she hadn't been out of the room since I left, and she needed me to hurry back to her before she developed claustrophobia. If Jackman was as good as I knew him to be, then Joy wouldn't have to hide for much longer, but I didn't tell her that because I didn't wanna get her hopes up. Instead, I reminded her not to stress and to make sure she ate something. Before I knew it, my flight was taxing, and I was airborne, at which time I reclined my seat and closed my eyes. I slept the entire flight, not awakening until we touched down, feeling completed rejuvenated. Tay was waiting on me in her black-on-black Denali in the pickup lane, and as soon as I hopped in, she pulled off.

"Tell me what happened," I demanded gently.

"I got a call from his daycare center saying that there were some government officials in the premise with documentation requesting to see Peanut's birth certificate. I went down there immediately, and as soon as I saw the ICE on their bulletproof vests, I knew that we had a problem. They told me that he would be returned to Paris until he was granted dual citizenship or given some type of temporary visa that allowed him to be in this country. What I don't understand is why this is happening *now*."

"Undoubtedly, Ant was betting on me to go and get our son, which meant that he would know my actual location, and he could either ambush me or go after Joy," I explained.

"Were you with her?"

The question was asked so low that the average muthafucka would've missed it, but I heard her loud and clear, and I knew the ramifications of a lie versus the truth.

"Yeah, I was with her, trying to hide her from Ant," I replied honestly.

"Hmmm... well, since you decided to tell me the truth, let me ask you another question, my dear husband. Who the fuck is your *other* baby mama?"

"Huh?" I replied, startled by the shift in direction and the venom that I heard in her voice.

"Don't play dumb, nigga, because your bitch dropped the ball when I texted her and asked if you were with her, and she responded by telling me that she would contact your other baby mama to see if you were with her. So, exactly how many bitches are you fucking on the side, Nate?"

For a moment, my mind scrambled because I thought that she knew Joy was pregnant, but then my mind caught the gear that it had slipped, and I realized that Tay was talking about Marissa. In all of the confusion, I'd forgotten that Marissa and Ava were still a secret I'd kept from my wife, but now, it was obvious that the time for telling that lie had passed.

"Okay, listen, I need you to calm down because I didn't cheat on you and get another bitch pregnant. The woman Joy was referring to is someone that I grew up with, and once I explain the whole thing, it'll make some sense," I said.

"I doubt that but start talking, nigga, because I really just wanna punch you in your shit," she replied in a deadly serious tone.

Regardless of whether or not she could beat me in a fight, I knew from past experiences that she would try me. Now wasn't the time for that though. I started from the beginning, which was my childhood, and told her everything about Marissa and Ava, including the night that I was thought to have murdered my own daughter and been gunned down by my baby mama. I finished the tale by pulling up the video of Marissa and Stuckey fucking to prove that I currently wasn't fucking with her at all. Tay was quiet the entire time that I'd been talking, and I thought that she'd have a million questions once I was done, but we rode in silence for the rest of the way to the house. When she pulled up, neither of us made a move to get out, and I could sense that she had more to say to me.

"You've gone through a lot to protect all of us... including Joy. I understand why you're so protective of me and Marissa, but you should've cut your losses with this bitch, Joy, by now. So, why haven't you, Nate? What's holding you to her?"

When she looked over at me, I saw the suspicion in her eyes, and I knew then that she had a gut feeling about the most hurtful secret that I was keeping. I knew that whether I lied to her or told the truth, I was still gonna hurt her because she already knew something in her soul. This realization made me feel like shit, but there was no time for me to wallow in my self pity.

"She's pregnant... And no matter what my intent was or how fucked up it is, that baby is innocent," I replied.

My response caused her eyes to fill up with tears immediately, and they spilled down her checks like water after the levee broke. Without another word, she got out of the SUV and went into the house. She left the front door open, but I didn't get out and follow her right away because

I knew that she needed a moment. While I gave her that, I checked in with Joy again and let her know that thanks to her big mouth, all of the cats were out of the bag. I didn't expect her to be remorseful or even give a fuck for real, but she surprised me by sending me a heartfelt apology almost immediately. Before I could respond to her though, I got a message from Jackman letting me know that my problem would be taken care of in a permanent way within a few hours. Hearing this gave me a feeling of relief, but I would save the celebratory actions until after I received confirmation that Ant was no longer walking amongst the living. I told Jackman to keep me posted, and then, I hopped out of the SUV to go find Tay. I honestly didn't wanna fight with her, but I would definitely fight for us because deep down, I still loved my wife very much, and I still wanted her. The problem was that I wanted it all though. It was dark in the foyer, but I could see light coming from the living room, so I closed the door and headed in that direction.

"Tay?" I called out.

When I came around the corner, I didn't know what to make of what I was seeing, but my brain quickly registered that there was a gun in one of Tay's hands and a phone in the other.

"Wh-What are you doing, bae?"

"Just showing all of my ladies out there how we really deal with lying, cheating, dirty dick ass niggas like you, sweetheart."

The smile on her face could be described as menacing, but that didn't mean that she was really gonna shoot me.

"Baby, let's just talk about…"

I felt the bullet rip through my left thigh just above the knee milliseconds before I heard the screaming boom from the barrel of her .45, and then, I hit the floor.

"Tay!" I growled angrily through clenched teeth.

"Yes, my love?"

"Stop and think this through because…"

Her second shot hit my left calf, and I felt the chunk of meat that the bullet shredded off the bone.

"Fuck!" I yelled, trying to struggle to my feet.

"Does it hurt, baby?" she asked, taunting me, as she moved closer.

It was clear to me that she'd lost her muthafuckin mind, but I knew that I still had to try and reason with her because I didn't have a gun to defend myself with.

"Baby, please don't do this. You know that I love you."

"And I love you too, Nate. I love you to death."

By now, she was standing right over top of me. When I looked up at her, I saw her intentions in her eyes, and I knew that my efforts at restoring calm were a lost cause. She stood over me and let off three quick shots that hit me center mass. The last thing that I heard before I lost consciousness was her hysterical laughter, and then the darkness closed in from all sides.

# Chapter 12

(Joy)
(One Week Later)

"I'm getting cabin fever just sitting in this bitch. When can I leave?" I asked, standing over Marissa, as she was reading something on her tablet at the kitchen table.

"You can leave when it's safe."

"Oh, my God, you keep saying that, but you have yet to explain how I'm still in any danger. It's been a whole week since a drone levelled the secret prison that Ant was in, so he's dead and gone by now," I said.

"We haven't confirmed that Ant is dead, and more importantly, we haven't figured out if his death cancelled the bounties on you and Nate. So, *until* we know that information, you're not safe, and you'll remain here. You're free to visit the pool and gym, just make sure to take at least two security people with you."

The urge that I had to scream and snatch this bitch up by her wig was so strong that I could feel the searing heat of angry bile rising in my throat. I resisted the urge, just barely, and only because I needed her. I took several deep breaths, and then I sat down next to her at the table.

"Have you heard anything else about what happened in North Carolina?" I asked in a gentler tone.

When she looked up at me, her stare was blank and faraway, but after a moment, she shook it off and focused on me.

"There's nothing in the house, not even Nate's body. The cops did find blood, and it's been confirmed that it's Nate's, but that's all we know."

"We know that he's dead. I mean, you saw the video and how many times she shot him, so since he's not laid up in the hospital, we have to more than consider the reality that he's really gone," I said, hating how the words sounded to my own ears.

"I hear what you're saying... but that's not a reality that I'm ready to accept yet. I need concrete proof, and nothing less will suffice. Not even the video that his wife posted."

"Speaking of his wife, how the fuck is it that she just vanished into thin air without a trace?" I asked, feeling more annoyed.

"I don't know, but now that Stuckey has Peanut settled with family in Atlanta, he's using all of his resources to find her. There's no evidence that she left the country, but no one knows because there's no trail to follow. All I know is that based on the crime scene, she dragged Nate's body to a vehicle and loaded him into it. Or at least that's what she staged it to look like. Traffic cam footage has proved useless because she was way out in the country, and without knowing what vehicle we're looking for, it was like looking for a needle in a stack of needles."

I heard the frustration in her tone and saw the exhaustion on her face, but I chose not to comment on either. It had been a fucked-up week for all of us, and I'd lost track of the ocean of tears that I'd cried. I knew that it was different for Marissa though because I had no doubt that the guilt was eating her alive inside. This wasn't something that she'd voiced, but it was obvious.

"Okay, so let's look at this from the best possible scenario and say that Nate is *not* dead. What's his wife's play?" I asked.

"I don't know, but she obviously lost her muthafuckin mind because she's the only person who would be dumb enough to shoot Nate and not kill him."

"You did it," I pointed out.

"Yeah, but that was because we had a plan, and I didn't actually put any holes in his muthafuckin' ass. His wife was out for blood, and she definitely got it."

"Alright, so let's say that she had buyer's remorse as he lay there bleeding out on the floor, and she decided to save him. Where could she take him to get treated and keep it lowkey?" I asked.

"That's the main question that I've been asking myself because she either got him help or dumped his body," she replied, looking at me with concern.

"What do you know about her? Does she have family in North Carolina?"

"Yeah, but she's originally from Pamplin, Virginia. Stuckey has been watching her people in both states without learning anything," she replied.

I thought about everything in silence for a moment, and suddenly, something dawned on me.

"She ain't tried to get her kid back?" I asked curiously.

"No, she hasn't."

"I can tell by the look on your face that you find this to be as weird as I do. What are you thinking though?" I asked.

"I'm thinking that no mother would do that, not even one hell bent on revenge, which means that she has to be *supremely* confident that her son is safe," Marissa replied, pulling out her phone.

"Who are you calling?"

"Stuckey because he needs to check to see if any inquiries were made with the French authorities about Nate's son's whereabouts," she replied.

"And then hopefully, the identity of the caller can be traced," I said, nodding, as I followed her train of thought.

I didn't wanna seem like I was hovering, so I got up with the intentions of taking her advice and going for a swim to relax a little. First, I returned to my room to slip into the swimsuit I'd bought the other day, and after grabbing my purse, I headed out toward the front door. Before my hand could grab the doorknob, it turned, and Ava was coming through the door. We'd barely seen each other in the last week, and I was all good with that, but in the back of my mind, I knew the confrontation was inevitable. Neither of us spoke, but the look of pure hatred in her eyes said all that was needed to be expressed.

"Excuse me," I said, waiting on her to step aside.

When she didn't immediately move, I knew that the inevitable confrontation had now arrived.

"I'm not 'bout to repeat myself, so I advise you to move," I said.

"Bitch, you only talking that shit because you think you're safe as long as you're pregnant, but I could give a fuck about that little bastard you're carrying. I'll smash you," she threatened, taking a step closer.

I may not have grown up in the streets, but I knew that one of the cardinal rules was that you didn't do no talking when action was required. For that reason, I didn't hesitate to drop my purse to step into the headbutt that I launched at her nose, and then I quickly followed up with a left-right punch combination that slung her blood against the wall. Naturally, she screamed, but none of that made me pause because I wrapped her hair around my left hand and knuckles while driving my right fist forcefully into her pretty face.

"Mom!" she screamed, trying in vain to get away.

"Un uh, don't holla for Mommy now, bitch," I growled while punching her harder.

I was just about to hit her with a knee to her face when I was suddenly snatched off of my feet and forcefully separated from her.

"Let me go!" I yelled, struggling against the security personnel.

He put me back on my feet, but he didn't turn me loose to allow me to get back on her ass.

"What the fuck is going on?" Marissa asked, coming around the corner fast like the house was on fire.

All it took was for her to get a good look at Ava's face, and she knew *exactly* what was going on.

"Take her to the penthouse next door and move her things as well," Marissa demanded, waving her hand dismissively in my direction.

I didn't resist when my arm was pulled. I simply chuckled, as I was led out the door and into another suite. If I had known that all I needed to do to get my own space was to whoop a bitch, I would've done that six days ago.

"Wait here while I get your other stuff," he demanded, passing me my purse.

I nodded my head like a good little girl, but my brain was already working like a good Swiss timepiece. I waited a slow fifteen seconds after I'd been left alone before I opened the door and peeked out into the hallway. Seeing that it was empty, I knew that this was my chance, and I didn't waste a second, as I dashed out into the hall and jumped in the elevator. The doors closed swiftly, and I was headed for the lobby, but it wasn't clear to me what I was gonna do when I got there. All I had on was my swimsuit and some flip-flops, which left me feeling damn near naked, but there was no time to hit up the gift shop here, so I headed out front. There were a few different Lyft drivers standing around conversing, but I chose to hop in the backseat of the young white girl who'd been smoking a blunt in private.

"Take me to the airport," I demanded.

"You paying cash or charge?"

"Charge," I replied, reaching for my phone in my purse.

"That'll cost you a $30 flat rate," she said, holding her own phone up.

Once I had my phone unlocked, I made the transaction by tapping my phone against hers, and she wasted no time pulling away from the hotel.

I knew that it wouldn't take long for Marissa to get the word that I'd disappeared, but I doubted that she'd put up as much of a fuss after the ass whooping I'd put on her daughter. Still, I needed to figure out what my next move was gonna be before I got to the airport. I knew that my car was parked in the long-term parking lot, which meant that I didn't have to take a flight out. That made more sense for me because if Marissa did decide to look for me or send her minions, then they'd check all of the flights going out first. I told the driver where to drop me off, and twenty minutes later, I was sliding behind the wheel of my Porsche.

Nate had told me that he'd left my keys under the driver's seat, and that was where I found them, but that automatically sent my mind spiraling back toward him. For a brief moment, I caught the faintest whiff of his scent inside the confines of my car, and I desperately wanted to hold on to it. In my soul, I felt like he was alive, but that faith didn't tell me in which direction to begin my search for him. I didn't wanna give Marissa a chance to catch up though, so I left the airport and headed southeast. I stopped for gas twice, but I drove through the night until I reached Kansas City where I got a motel room.

I paid in cash, made sure to close the curtains once I was in the room, and then I collapsed on the soft mattress. Sleep was immediate, but it wasn't my friend because all of my dreams had Nate in them. It was like my brain had been programmed to remember every single detail about him and I, and that shit made my heart hurt. I finally awoke in the middle of the night in a cold sweat. I looked at my phone and saw that it was 2 a.m., but surprisingly, I didn't have any missed calls from Marissa. I knew that I'd have to wait until at least sunrise before I ordered myself clothes or got anything else done, so I didn't even bother getting out of bed.

I just laid there, looking at the ceiling, until sleep spun the block again and pulled me back under. This time around, my dreams weren't a highlight reel of my relationship with Nate. It was a Mexican standoff with Nate in the middle of a triangle made up of me, Marissa, and his wife. No one was talking, but it was obvious that we were all waiting on him to make a decision. When his eyes locked with mine, I felt my heart stop, and then, I was snatched from my sleep by the sound of my phone ringing.

"Hello?" I answered in a raspy voice with my eyes still closed.

"Where are you, and what the fuck happened?"

I recognized Stuckey's voice, and I instantly got annoyed at being questioned by him.

"Stop talking to me like you're my daddy, nigga, cause you ain't. And what happened was that Ava kept popping her shit like she wanted to do her big one, so I had to let her know that shit wasn't sweet for real," I replied, swinging my feet to the floor blindly.

"You didn't have to do all of that, Joy, and that shit ain't helping the situation. Everyone got enough to worry about without your extra drama, so take your ass back to the hotel," he demanded.

I pulled the phone away from my ear and looked at it because I knew that I wasn't hearing what I thought I'd heard. I hit the end button as soon as that nigga started talking again and dropped my phone on the bed, as I headed for the shower. I took a blistering hot, twenty-minute escape, and then, I threw my swimsuit back on because it was looking nice and warm outside of the bathroom window. I noticed the dozen missed calls I had, as I grabbed my phone and car keys, but I ignored them because undoubtedly, they were from Stuckey. I left the room, hopped in my car, and headed for the nearest fast-food place, which happened to be McDonald's.

Once I had my food, I got back on the highway, headed farther southeast, only now I had an idea of ultimately where I'd end up. The conversation that Marissa and I had about Nate's wife not being too concerned about her child was playing back in my mind, and it was giving me an idea of how to draw her out. To my way of thinking, the only way for Tay to know that Peanut was safe was if she'd seen that for herself. She would only trust Stuckey so far. My confidence in this was the reason that my destination was Atlanta, and it only took me six hours to enter the city limits.

When I got there, I found a hotel to hole up in, and once I got there, I ordered clothes and a MacBook pro tablet to work with. I doubted that Stuckey would have Peanut in plain sight, which meant that it could take a while to find him, and that was time that I didn't have to waste. When I called him, the phone rang twice before it was answered.

"Have you come to your senses yet?" he asked.

"Not if you're talking about me going back to Colorado and sitting on my hands, doing nothing. I can't and won't do that because I need to find your brother. Now, are you gonna help or not?"

His response was to go silent, but I knew that he hadn't hung up; he was simply thinking.

"What do you have in mind?" he asked finally.

"Before shit went bad in Colorado, Marissa and I had been talking about how Tay disappeared, and she didn't seem too concerned about her son. I believe that's because she's close by and has her eyes on her son."

"I mean, it's possible because she knows my family, but I don't got her just sitting around knowing that she's wanted for murder," he replied.

"Technically, she's only wanted for questioning because you can't prove murder without a body, and she can easily say it was a hoax. Despite her recording the shooting and posting it on social media, she never shows her face. Trust me, I've watched the video more times that I care to admit or remember."

"Okay... so you believe that she's somewhere in Atlanta, hiding in the shadows. How does that theory help you when you're across the country?" he asked.

"I'm not across the country. I'm in Atlanta. And the info helps me because I'm betting that her seeing me with her son will bring her out into the light."

"Wait, your plan is to use yourself as bait to piss Tay off? Have you not grasped how crazy this woman is?" he asked in disbelief.

"No, I grasp it, but I'm betting that she won't do anything in front of her son. It's worth the gamble," I insisted.

I could feel the hesitation, and I knew that it was for good reason because if anything happened to any of us, he'd have to carry the guilt. He was already carrying a heavy load.

"Joy, I pray that you know what you're doing because this shit is crazy."

"I know it's crazy, but there's no other way. I need to know if Nate's really dead."

# Chapter 13

### (Nate)

The extreme pain that I felt made me believe that I'd finally reached hell for all the sins that I'd committed, but something told me that I was still above ground. At least for the moment. It hurt more each time I tried to move, so I laid there and attempted to take mental stock of my injuries. In order to do that, I first had to remember what happened, and that hurt about as much as the gunshots. I'd always known how crazy and dangerous Tay could be, but I never thought that she'd actually shoot the shit out of me. Granted, only the first two shots were live rounds, but the three rubber bullets she'd hit me with at close range had still been powerful enough to break a few ribs and knock me the fuck out. Every time I took a breath, I could feel the cracks in my ribs, but my left leg hurt more, and I knew that walking with a limp was my destiny.

"You can open your eyes because I know you're conscious," Tay said.

Her voice came from somewhere on my right, but when I opened my eyes, I looked at the ceiling and not at her.

"Awww, you're mad. Don't be because you had it coming, and shit could've been much, much worse for your trifling ass," she said.

I wanted to respond, but I bit a hole in my tongue because I knew that provoking her would be dumb on my part.

"Where am I?"

"At a house that I rented not far from our son," she replied.

"We're in Spain? You smuggled me out of the country? How long have I been out?" I asked, feeling a touch of panic.

"Spain? Nigga, please. We're in Atlanta. If you told Stuckey to meet you in Spain, then he didn't follow your directions, but I guess with everyone thinking that you're dead, I could see why he'd change his plans."

"You let everyone think that I was dead? Why?" I asked, finally turning my head to lock eyes with her.

"Because per your vows, you belong to *me*, and I'm not obligated to share you with a muthafuckin' soul. That includes illegitimate kids and baby mamas."

I wanted to ask her to be reasonable, but I knew that would only piss her off.

"How long?" I asked again.

"You've been in and out of consciousness for about eight days, but that was probably for the best given the amount of pain you would've been in. The two shots to your left leg went straight through, and with just a little skin graft, you look as good as new. The bullet holes were lasered closed, so the pain that you feel in that area is nothing more than a phantom thing. Unfortunately, your ribs are broken, and there's no magical repair for that."

"At least you didn't let me bleed out," I mumbled, averting my eyes back to the ceiling.

"Trust me, I considered leaving you to your fate, but I know how much that would hurt our son."

I started to say some smart shit, but there was no point. Instead, my mind shifted toward escaping because I most definitely had to get away from this crazy ass woman. I struggled to sit up in the bed, fighting the immense pain that had sweat popping up above my upper lip, while I willed myself not to lose consciousness again.

"No need to overdo it, sweetheart. There's nowhere that you have to be at the moment," she said, sounding way too happy about my limited mobility.

"Unless you found a way to kill Ant, then I most definitely have someplace to be because no one is safe while he's alive."

"I don't know where Ant is, but he wouldn't be caught dead in Atlanta," she replied.

"Right, Atlanta. That must mean that Peanut is with Stuckey's side of the family," I surmised, struggling to my feet.

It wasn't lost on me that I was completely naked, but I ignored that, as I staggered and stumbled to the bathroom. It had never felt so good to piss in all my life, and by the time I was done with that, I had a plan taking shape in my mind. When I came out of the bathroom, Tay was still sitting in the same chair in the corner of the room, tapping away on her phone.

"Ain't no time to be playing on Instagram," I said.

"Why not? Ever since I shot you, I've gone viral and become instafamous with very little blowback from the police because they can't figure out if it was a hoax. Plus, I was smart enough not to show my face. So, I've gotta make time for my fans."

"Your fans? Bitch, please. Those are just some crazy bitter bitches who've been cheated on, or they're just miserable enough to enjoy you shooting your own husband," I said, making my way back to the queen-sized bed.

"I guess that I should thank you for making me one of those bitter bitches," she said.

"That was never my intent, and you should know that. I can completely understand you being mad about Joy because I used faulty logic, but for you to actually shoot me for some shit that happened *before* you and I were together was crazy as fuck."

"I didn't shoot you for actually having a grown ass kid that you kept a secret. I shot you for keeping her a *secret!* You're *my* nigga, and we're married, which means there should be *no* secrets between us. There damn sure shouldn't be no secret fucking kids!" she replied heatedly.

I had no sound logic to counter her argument, so I kept my mouth shut and gave her a few moments to calm back down before she got it in her mind to shoot me again.

"Look, I'm not trying to argue with you, so why don't you just tell me what your plan is here?"

"I don't really know. It was impulse that made me shoot you, and I've just been kinda making shit up as I go along, while I waited on you to heal," she replied honestly.

"I'm healed enough to move around, so we need to come up with some type of plan," I insisted, looking over at her.

"Okay, I'm listening."

"Well, first, we gotta let certain people know that I'm not dead for the second time," I said.

"I disagree. I think you need to remain invisible this time if your goal is really to eliminate the threat to you and us."

For a moment, I simply stared at her, trying to figure out if she was on some selfish shit or some survival shit. In the end, I realized that it was both, but that didn't make her wrong.

"Okay. Then, we take Peanut and disappear until I get word about Ant or until that's dealt with once and for all," I said.

"What's your plan to deal with Ant?"

"I contracted someone to blow up the prison that the Feds had him moved to," I replied honestly.

She stared at me for a few moments, and then she got out of her seat and came to sit beside me.

"I saw this last week, but I didn't know that it was your doing," she said, pulling up some news video footage on her phone.

I watched the report of the drone strike in Louisiana that was claimed by some terrorist group in the Middle East, and I smiled because Jackman had left the prison looking like a hollowed-out building in Kyiv, Russia. My nigga had definitely earned the money that I'd paid him.

"Were there any survivors?" I asked.

"Not even the K-9s patrolling the grounds."

"Aww, poor little doggies," I replied, laughing softly despite the pain it caused me.

"So, now that you know Ant is dead, what's your next move?"

"I need to locate his most trusted associates and kill them too, just in case they've sworn to avenge him. All of his clean money is in Joy's possession, so now she'll inherit the rest and thereby control the empire," I said, liking the decisive advantage that provided.

"Good, that means the little bitch has the money to get an abortion."

My thoughts immediately came to a screeching halt, as I digested what my wife had just said.

"What?" I asked.

"You heard me, Nathan. Either she gets rid of that kid or this marriage is over over. I'll take my son and disappear, while you play house with your whores," she replied, getting up and moving back to her seat.

"It don't just work like that. I have no right to tell that woman to kill her baby, and even if I did, I doubt that she'd listen."

"Then you *make* her listen because I promise you that when I shoot her muthafuckin' ass, won't nary bullet be made of rubber. I've got special bullets that explode on impact for that bitch," she said, sneering maliciously.

This was a side of my wife that I'd never seen before, which made me understand that I needed to proceed with caution. When she'd first said that our marriage was over back when I'd first went to see her in North Carolina, I'd thought that all she needed was some time to figure things out, but the look in her eyes now told me that time couldn't heal these wounds I'd caused. I doubted that anything could.

"I'll talk to her," I said, sighing heavily.

"You should probably have that conversation sooner than later. In the meantime, now that you're awake, we can go get our son. There's clothes for you in the closet, so get dressed, and I'll fix something to eat," she replied, getting up and leaving the room.

It took me a few minutes to work up my nerve because I knew that as soon as I started moving, the pain was gonna come instantly. When I finally stood up, I thought that I was gonna pass out, but the wave passed, and I was allowed to walk it off somewhat.

It took me damn near ten minutes to get dressed, and then I walked slowly up the hallway, following the smell of sausage and eggs. The kitchen was what one would describe as cozy with a small table up against the wall next to the refrigerator. I took a seat slowly, still struggling to breathe around the pain, but the feeling was somewhat better because my body had loosened up a little more.

"I need to call Stuckey," I said.

She spared me a brief glance over her shoulder, and that was the only indication that she heard me.

"Tay, I'll make sure he knows not to tell anyone that I'm still alive."

She still didn't give a verbal response, so I left the topic alone for the moment and just let her cook. A few minutes later, she slid a plate in front of me and dropped a fork beside it.

"I thought about spitting in it, but I controlled my petty," she said, as she went back to the stove.

For a moment, I just stared at the food on the plate in front of me, but finally, I picked up the fork and began to eat slowly. The immediate reaction from my stomach was a standing ovation, and I had to stop the moan of satisfaction that wanted to leap from my throat. I couldn't remember the last time that I'd ate, but based on my body's reaction, I could guess that it had been a while. I definitely felt smaller, so I knew that I'd lost some weight. I tried to eat as slow as possible to avoid the pain, but my ferocious appetite overrode that logic, and within a few minutes, my plate was completely empty. I wanted more, but I could feel the tightness of my stomach, and I didn't wanna overdo it.

"Damn," Tay said when she turned around and saw what I'd done.

I didn't say anything. I just pushed my plate away. She sat down with her plate and began to eat while watching me closely. I met her gaze head on, wondering what she was thinking because, in a lot of ways, this woman had become a stranger to me.

"You're different," I said.

"What was your first clue, the bullet in your left thigh?"

"Nah, because I've always known that you were crazy but sitting here with you now, just looking at you, I realized how much you changed and how little I know about you now," I replied.

"You say that like you wanna know me or something, but I doubt that we can go back to being best friends."

"Why not?" I asked, genuinely curious to hear her point of view.

"Why do you think, Nate? There was only *one* thing that could destroy everything that we'd built, and not only did you do that, but you actually got the bitch pregnant. Do you even comprehend how much that hurts me? How do you expect me to get past that? How do you expect me to ever trust you when you've been lying to me for years?"

Her questions were valid, but I didn't have an answer for any of them. I wanted to blame all of my decisions on Ant, but the reality was that it was my bullshit and my obsession that had put me in this situation. Analytical thinking only worked so much in emotionally charged situations, so all the sense that I thought I had wasn't counting for shit because I'd only caused pain to those that I cared about. The current question was what came now?

"I have no right to ask for your trust or understanding, so I guess all either of us can do is focus on Peanut," I said.

Her nod was subtle, but the stress in her eyes was more than obvious. I hated myself for hurting the one woman who'd done the most for me and meant the most to me. Deep down, I knew that I'd always hate myself.

"You need to reach out to your brother," she said, sliding my phone across the table to me.

I caught it, and then, I dialed his number.

"Who the fuck is this?" he asked, answering after the first ring.

"Who the fuck you think it is, nigga?" I countered.

"Thank God you're alive. After seeing that video, I'd thought that she'd really put your ass in the ground for your bullshit."

"It felt like I died, trust me. The last three shots were dummy bullets that hurt like a bitch, and at such a close range, they broke a few of my ribs," I said.

"Sounds painful. Where are you though, bruh?"

"I'm not far away, which is why I'm calling you. I'm coming for my son, and then we're gonna disappear for a little while. You can't tell *anyone* that I'm alive, not even Marissa," I said.

"That's crazy work. Why are you keeping the fact that you're alive a secret? That nigga, Ant, is dead dead, and there's been no chatter about the bounty he put on you and Joy surviving his death, which means that you're good," he said.

His question caused me to look across the table at my wife, who was chewing her food slowly and watching me. I knew that she couldn't hear the whole conversation, but undoubtedly, she was guessing was Stuckey was saying.

"I'm aware that Ant is dead, and I'm still making sure that there's not a price on my heads before I announce to the world that I'm back outside. Plus, my wife and I need time to get reconnected," I replied while staring directly into her eyes.

"I hear you, bruh. So, I'mma send you the address to my aunt's house in Atlanta where Peanut is and just hit me up when you get where it's safe."

"I got you," I replied, disconnecting the call.

"Do you think he'll keep his mouth shut?" she asked.

"I don't know, but either way, it don't matter because I'm gonna have facial reconstruction again to change my entire look," I replied.

"I miss your old face," she blurted out.

I didn't say anything. I just gave her a crooked smile.

"Stuckey is gonna send the address where Peanut is, and then we can go get him."

"I don't need the address. I told you that he's right down the street. Come on, let's go," she said, pushing her plate away and standing up.

It took me longer to rise, but I made it to my feet, and I followed her lead outside.

"You got a new ride," I said, admiring the black-on-black Dodge Ram TRX sitting a few feet away in the driveway.

"Yeah, it made me feel good to blow some of your hard-earned money just because I could."

I didn't say anything because I knew that she was baiting me to cuss her ass the fuck out. I struggled to climb up into the passenger side of the four-door cab, but when I finally made it, she cranked the engine and pulled off. We'd only been riding for a few minutes before I got a call from Stuckey. I started to ignore it since Tay knew where we were going, but something told me to answer the call.

"Yeah, what's up?"

"You need to brace yourself for a serious conflict," he warned.

"What the fuck are you talking 'bout?"

"I'm talking about your wife coming face to face with your mistress."

"How the fuck would that be possible when she should be across the country?" I asked.

"I know goddamn well that ain't who I think it is," Tay said from beside me.

I looked over at her, and then I followed her gaze out the front windshield to the front lawn of the house that we'd just stopped in front of. The sight of Joy running around the yard with Peanut sent a jolt of panic and adrenaline through my body because I knew that this shit was about to go bad.

"Remind me to shoot you," I said, hanging up on Stuckey.

"The only person who's about to get shot is that bitch playing with my son," Tay vowed, throwing the truck in park and hopping out.

Suddenly, the pain in my body was forgotten because I knew that it would take immediate action in order to save Joy's life.

# Chapter 14

### (Joy)

"I'm gonna get you!" I said, laughing, as I chased after Peanut.

His childish squealing and high-pitched laughter were melodies that I longed to hear from my own child, and it dawned on me that despite the circumstances, I couldn't wait to be a mom. This realization made me miss Nate even more because our baby was the last piece of him that this world would ever have.

"Bitch, get the fuck away from my son!"

The sound of a female's voice yelling at me startled me out of the moment I'd been having, and I looked up to see Nate's very pissed off wife headed toward me.

"Mommy!" Peanut squealed, immediately shifting directions to head toward her.

He was moving just as fast as his little legs would carry him until he suddenly stopped dead in his tracks.

"Daddy! Daddy!" he yelled, jumping up and down before taking off at a different angle.

When I looked left and saw Nate, my heart completely stopped, and I felt my eyes fill with tears that I was helpless to fight. It was clear to see by how slowly he was moving that he was still injured, but that didn't stop him from catching his son when he leaped toward him. It was a moment of beauty, but my instincts made my focus shift back to Tay, who was still moving in my direction. Without hesitation, I pulled the Glock .42 I'd purchased out of my back pocket, and I held it out to my side in a way that allowed her to clearly see it. Her steps faltered, and she glanced back at the truck quick enough for me to know that was where her gun was.

"I don't wanna do this in front of your son," I said, keeping the pistol pressed against my thigh.

"Then you shouldn't have brought your ho ass here," she replied heatedly.

"Honestly, I was just playing a hunch that Nate was still alive since his body was never recovered. I'm only here for him," I explained calmly.

"Do you not understand that he's still *my* muthafuckin' husband, bitch? That means that you don't just get to pop up like we're sharing him because I damn sure ain't 'bout to do that. He used you. Now get over it and have an abortion so that you can go back to your miserable fucking life."

The nastiness of her tone didn't surprise me because as a woman, I'd probably feel the same way, but the fact that she thought that I was gonna kill my child did baffle the fuck out of me. I looked at Nate to see if he'd put this crazy idea in her head, but the plea for peace in his eyes made me feel like this wasn't his idea. For a moment, I didn't say anything, but then, I pulled the slide on my pistol to chamber the first round, and I leveled the gun at her.

"Say that shit again, bitch. I dare you. Tell me to kill my baby again, and I swear on my little one's soul that I'mma drop your ass right here, and then I'll be raising both of our kids," I threatened, resting my right index finger on the double triggers.

She stared at me with so much harnessed hatred that I thought that she might actually make the fatal mistake that would get her ass deaded on this bright green grass, but she didn't say shit.

"Put it away, Joy," Nate said, moving slowly toward me.

I didn't do what he said until I knew that my point had been made, and even then, I kept it tucked in the front of my pants for easy access. When Nate stopped in front of me, I looked up at him, and I couldn't stop the tears from spilling.

"Why-Why didn't you tell me that you were alive?" I asked, barely controlling the urge to openly sob.

"I just fully regained consciousness," he replied.

Hearing this made me wanna shoot this bitch, Tay, again because she'd known that he wasn't dead, but she'd kept that important info to herself on some selfish shit. I resisted the urge for violence though, but I made up my mind that I wasn't letting this nigga out of my sight again.

"We need to go," I said.

"Go? Go where and why?"

"I don't care where we go, but we need not be out in the open where our enemies could run down on us," I explained.

"Joy, I don't know if you know, but Ant is dead. We're safe."

"That's probably what your brother told you, but my knowledge is a little more intimate given that I'm the one in charge of all of the affairs controlled by Ant. Ant's death has created a power struggle that's epic because everyone had always assumed that my mother would outlive him and assume his position. Were it not for the money that he put on my head, I could probably make his people respect my position of authority, but they knew that Ant wasn't fucking with me which means they shouldn't either," I said.

I watched as he processed what I was saying, but I made sure to keep my eyes on Tay too just in case she decided to make a slick move toward her truck.

"Okay, so what's your plan?" he finally asked.

"I don't have a plan... I just have you," I confessed, praying that I was right about the latter.

He glanced over his shoulder and looked at his wife, and I could feel his mind working to formulate a plan that could benefit all of us. I didn't envy his position.

"Tay, come here," he demanded gently.

I saw her hesitation out of my peripheral, but I kept my eyes focused on Nate's face, trying to guess which way he was going with this.

"What the fuck do you want, nigga, and don't say no dumb shit like a threesome because I'll definitely dead this bitch right here, right now," she threatened.

"Bitch!" Peanut said.

"Watch your mouth around him, sweetheart, and you know that I'm not 'bout to *ever* suggest no crazy ass shit like that. I just need you to know what's going on because from now on, there can be no secrets," he replied, passing their son to her.

For a moment, none of the adults spoke to each other, and the only sounds were those of Peanut talking to his mom, while he played with her face. It was clear that she missed him as much as he'd missed her, and that made me glad that I'd trusted my instincts about not simply taking him and leaving.

"What do I need to know?" she asked, sounding much less hostile now.

When Nate nodded at me, I began to explain what I'd told him word for word, and then I waited on her response.

"Do you think that whoever the defacto leader of Ant's criminal enterprise turns out to be will come after you?" she asked, directing her question to Nate.

"They don't have a choice because there's no doubt that they know that the reason Ant disowned Joy is because she was fucking with me. Based on that, we can only assume that they know she's pregnant by me, which makes killing her sweeter for them and more necessary. So, they know that they gotta kill me because I'm *definitely* gonna get my lick back," he stated passionately.

The way that he was determined to protect me made my pussy throb and drip, but I kept my mind focused on the tasks that lay ahead.

"I don't understand why it's necessary to come after you just because of her though," she replied.

"Aside from her carrying the heir to the throne, there's the fact that they could be scared that Joy will turn everything over to me. My name and work speak for themselves," he stated arrogantly.

"Okay, so what is it that you really want from me, Nathan? You already know that I give no fucks about her dying, but if anyone kills your muthafuckin' ass, it's gonna be me," she said seriously.

"What I want is for you to be understanding of the danger that we're facing, and I want you to take Peanut and leave the country. No arguments. I just need you to go," he explained.

"And leave you here to die? What type of bitch do you think I am?" she asked, looking at him like he was crazy, stupid, or both.

"Bitch!" Peanut squealed again.

"He's not gonna die. I'm not gonna let that happen," I stated confidently.

"And I'd trust you with his life because?" she asked sarcastically while locking eyes with me.

"Because I need him alive as much as you do, so in the interest of my own selfishness, I'm not gonna let shit happen to him."

"You know that the only way for me to focus is if you and Peanut are safe," he said.

"Yeah, nigga, and the last time that you told me that, you popped up with more kids, and you were unfaithful as fuck," she replied, still looking at me with hostility.

I knew better than to comment on what she said, so I kept my mouth shut.

"Baby, I hear what you're saying, and nothing that I say will make you feel good about leaving, but it has to be done this way. If there is another way then tell me, and we'll all figure it out," he offered.

The silence that hung in the air following his statement spoke volumes, and I imagined that this was pissing her off even more. The truth was what it was though.

"Peanut, give your daddy a hug and kiss goodbye so that we can go," she said, handing their son back to Nate.

While father and son shared that moment, Tay stepped toe to toe with me and spoke softly.

"If you get him killed, there won't be anywhere on Earth where you can hide from me. I promise."

"Understood," I replied, nodding.

For a moment, she just stared at me, and then she turned around to Nate. I chose to give them their moment as a family, so I turned and went to my car that was parked on a side street. When I slid behind the wheel, I had to will myself not to watch because I knew that I'd only succeed in breaking my own heart. It was confusing to me how I could still have so much love for a man who'd blatantly deceived and manipulated me, but that was my truth. I loved him. I accepted that, and I knew that it would benefit all of us for me to tap into that love and think as his equal to help keep us all from a premature death.

With this in mind, I pulled my phone out and texted Stuckey to get some information on the man that we were going to see first. I knew that Nate would be too stubborn and proud to use his brother's help, but I understood that right now Stuckey was a necessary evil and a means to an end. Plus, I knew that Stuckey was all too eager to do anything in order to make amends for the way he had betrayed his brother over some pussy. Little did he know, there was no making up for what he'd done. Nate wasn't the type of nigga to forgive and forget but based on how he'd played the game with Ant, I could definitely attest to the fact that he was more than patient when it came to revenge.

Within a few moments, I got the thumbs up emoji from Stuckey, and that started the clock in my mind. By the time Nate climbed into my passenger seat, I'd chartered a plane for Peanut and Tay, and I was mentally planning my next move.

"Send this info to Tay," I said, passing him my phone.

He took a minute to read the charter confirmation, and then he looked over at me.

"Thank you," he said, sounding genuinely surprised, as he sent the text.

I gave him a curt nod before I started the car and pulled off.

"Where we going?" he asked.

"The next nigga in line for the coveted throne that Ant sat on is a light skin nigga named Gooch, and he's up in Virginia. So, that's where we're headed."

"What do you know about him?" he asked, turning in the seat to give me his undivided attention.

"Not a lot for real. He's in his early thirties, and he's been running around Virginia reppin' Watts Bounty Hunters, which is some type of Blood set based in California. When I googled the nigga, I found some petty crimes, and he's a registered sex offender," I replied.

"What's the link between him and Ant? I know that Ant represented the East Coast Bloods, and I doubt that he had any use for a sex offender."

"I don't really know because I only saw the nigga, Gooch, one time at this huge meeting that Ant had put together. Ant was about his money though, so I'd bet that their affiliation either involved money or dope," I replied.

"We need to figure out everything that we can and formulate a plan of action."

I knew that his next thought was Stuckey, but he was way too proud to say it. Now wasn't the time to be proud though.

"I've already sent the name to your brother, and he's looking into him right now."

"And when exactly did you and my brother get so muthafuckin' friendly?" he asked, immediately sounding hostile.

"We're not friendly, so stop thinking what you're thinking. The only reason that he's helping me is because he knows you'll blame him if anything happens to me. Plus, I spared Ava."

"What the fuck do you mean you spared Ava? What don't I know?" he asked rapidly.

"Ain't shit really happen. She just started feeling herself a little too much, and she kept trying to talk to me with her chest. So, I gave her a good ass whooping, and then I left."

I could see him shaking his head out of my peripheral vision, but deep down, I knew that he understood how obnoxious his daughter could be. We rode in silence for another half an hour, but I didn't get the sense that he was mad at me. If anyone could understand that shit just happened sometimes, it was him. I wasn't gonna force him to talk though because he was a grown ass man who definitely knew how to use his words. I just kept my focus on the road in front of us.

"How's the baby?" he asked softly.

"Wh-What?"

"The baby... our baby, how is it?" he clarified.

"I mean, fine, I guess, but I haven't exactly had time to go to the doctors for a checkup."

"I can understand that. Just try to be careful," he said.

When I looked over at him, I could see the genuine concern in his eyes, and it hit me with more power than my sexual desires for him. I didn't know what to say though, so I kept my mouth shut. When I got us on the open highway, I was able to let my Porsche breathe, and I didn't drop below one hundred fifty miles per hour until we crossed the Tennessee state line. Once we got to Nashville, I found us an Airbnb to rent, and we pulled up to rest for a little while.

"I'm gonna take a shower, and you order the food," I said once we were inside the two-story cottage style house.

I didn't wait for a response. I just found the master bedroom and headed for the relief of hot water. I didn't reemerge for half an hour, and as soon as I opened the door, I could smell the spicy chicken wings calling to me. I wasted no time throwing on a Terry cloth robe and heading downstairs where I found Nate sitting in front of the eighty-inch flat screen TV, eating pizza and wings while watching a movie.

"What movie is that?" I asked, sitting beside him and grabbing a slice of pepperoni pizza for myself.

"A gangsta movie on TUBI called *I'mma Die Bout Mine*. Have you seen it?"

"Nah, but I've seen the prequel which is *The Bossman's Daughters*. They're all based off of these dope ass hood books, and the story is good as fuck," I replied, getting comfortable.

"Okay, well, I'm green to all of it, so don't tell me *shit!*"

I chuckled at his seriousness, but I didn't spoil the movie for him. Instead, I stuffed my face full of pizza and wings until my stomach felt like it would burst, and then I carried my ass back upstairs to the bed that was calling me. As soon as my head hit the pillow, I felt sleep overpowering my eyelids, forcing them down and forcing me to follow.

The peacefulness of sleep didn't last long though because I could feel Nate gently shaking me awake.

"Wh-What's wrong?" I asked, still half asleep.

"Your phone," he said, holding it up in front of my face.

It took me a few moments to focus on the screen, but I eventually got the text message open, and I was able to read what Stuckey had sent.

"Your brother sent the info on the nigga, Gooch."

"What else did he say?"

"Nothing, why?" I asked.

In response to my question, Nate pushed his phone at me, and I was able to see that he'd been watching a CNN news report. I hit the button to start from the beginning, and the first thing that I heard was that Stuckey was no longer serving as interim director of the CIA, and Marissa wasn't the chief of police.

"Is this because of the video I posted?"

"In a small part, yes, but it's mainly to do with the fact that the government wants me brought in," he replied.

"Brought in? For what?"

"I'm guessing because they feel like I know too much, or I've done too much to just get a free pass," he replied, nonplussed.

"So, what would they want from you, Nathan?" I pressed, no longer the least bit interested in sleep.

He was quiet for a moment, but then he looked me squarely in the eyes.

"I'd say that they probably want me dead because a dead man tells no tales."

# Chapter 15

(Nate)
(One Day Later)

It took many hours of serious convincing for me to get Joy to stay put in the Airbnb while I came to Virginia and did some in person recon on the nigga, Gooch. During the drive up here, I'd called in some old favors for info on ole boy, but there really wasn't a lot to go on. His name wasn't ringing any bells in the streets of Virginia's seven cities, and nobody in northern Virginia had ever heard of the nigga. A couple of niggas that I'd done time with knew who he was, but they described him as a goofy type, which hardly made him the one qualified to take over the empire that Ant had built. I did hear from different people that Gooch was trained to go, so I couldn't underestimate his willingness to go to war for that top spot and all the prestige that came with it. The goal right now was to find his weakness and exploit it.

Once I finally made it to Richmond, Virginia, I stopped at an IHOP to get some breakfast and use their Wi-Fi to dig a little deeper into my newest opp. I found several news reports talking about the violence that Gooch's gang members had inflicted, but I wasn't seeing his name in any of the specific accounts. That could've meant that he was just smart enough to be with the shit and not get caught. This painted a picture of how I needed to go about dealing with him, but first, I had to find him.

Joy's connections weren't turning up any locations for him, but it was known that he'd been released from the Virginia DOC into the custody of some rehab facility. This was supposed to be some type of sex offender program, which made me think less of the nigga, but I kept my focus on picking up on his trail.

I ordered some food while I searched for more info on the rehabs equipped for his particular problem, and then I called them on some official type shit. It took me three different calls to find the right place, and when I did, I was told that he'd been released already. I thought that put me back at square one until I was told that he was monitored by twenty-four-hour GPS location, and that made me laugh. It was impossible for a nigga to be invisible when he had a GPS tracker on his dumb ass.

Now that I knew how I was gonna find him, I reached out to Jackman to see if he was still up to earn some more money. He responded immediately with the thumbs up emoji and asked for the details. Once I filled him in, he sent me a message back, saying that he'd take this job at a discounted rate because it was easy work. Half a million would get it done quickly and swiftly. I sent the money, but I fucked with Jackman enough to warn him against sleeping on any opp. I didn't want him getting killed his damn self. He sent me the crying laughing emoji, and then he explained why he wasn't really worried. His plan was to simply report to the top dogs in Gooch's gang and let them know that his sex offense was for him making a little boy suck his dick. From there, it would only be a matter of time before they handled it.

I sent him a message back that said, "well played," and then, I turned my attention to what I considered to be a personal problem. I sent Stuckey a message and told him to meet me at my safehouse in Maryland so that we could talk and form a strategy. He readily agreed. With that done, I sent Joy a message and told her that all of our problems were almost over, and I'd be back in Tennessee by tomorrow to get her so that we could leave the country. Of course, her curiosity was piqued, but I refused to say more over the open airwaves. Her solution was to tell me that she'd checked out of the Airbnb, and she was getting a car to bring her to my spot in Maryland. I started to tell her no, but I didn't really see a problem with her knowing what the next move was, and it saved me time. I made our travel arrangements to have us gone within seventy-two hours, contacted my favorite doctor and told him where to meet me, and then, I paid my bill and got on the move to Maryland.

The drive to Maryland only took me a couple hours, and that allowed me to spend the rest of the afternoon making moves and countermoves. I really wanted to let Ava know that I was okay, but I knew that she would go straight to her mom with that information, and I didn't need that. Me being dead was safer for everyone right now. It was about 8 p.m. when Stuckey finally arrived, and I calmly opened the door to let him in.

"Sup, bruh?" he said, stepping inside.

I let him get both feet planted inside the house before I smacked him over the head with my Smith & Wesson .45. He crumbled to the floor like a drunk at a house party. I dragged him downstairs into the basement and then tied his arms to ropes hanging from the ceiling's cross beam. Once that was done, I made sure to gag him and cut his clothes off. I sat in a chair not far from him with a bucket at his feet and a mini blow torch in my hand. After about ten minutes, he started moaning groggily, signaling that he was coming around to consciousness, so I removed the gag.

"Wh-What the fuck did you hit me for?"

"Is that a serious question? Did you really think that you wouldn't have to answer for fucking Marissa, bruh?" I asked calmly.

"Come on, bruh. We ain't never let no pussy come in between us."

The way that he categorized my baby mama like she was some nothing ass bitch pissed me off and forced me to shoot him in his left foot. The sound of screams was music to my ears.

"Marissa ain't just a piece of pussy, my nigga, so I suggest you don't say that again," I warned, tucking my pistol and switching the blow torch to my other hand.

"O-Okay, just chill."

"Oh, I'm chillin, but I can't have you bleeding all over my shit," I said, grabbing ahold of his leg, as I fired up the torch.

He struggled, and it hurt my still healing ribs, but I pushed through the pain to get to the pleasure of hearing his screams again. I made sure the wound was closed before I turned him loose and took a seat again. While he moaned and cried, I pulled out my phone and sent a text to find out what time my doctor would arrive, and then, I asked Joy the same question. Within minutes, I had replies of one saying they were a half an hour out, and the other was less than fifteen minutes away.

"Okay, we ain't got a lot of time, so I'mma need you to stop whining like a bitch and answer my questions."

"F-Fuck you," he mumbled.

I started to shoot him again, but now wasn't the time for that.

"All you gotta do is answer my questions, and I promise that this will be painless. Tell me why you're no longer director of the CIA."

"There's an internal investigation going on because they're not sure that I haven't been helping you. Not to mention, the whole sex tape fiasco your precious Joy leaked," he replied.

I'd figured as much, but his confirmation let me know that my plan was actually gonna work perfectly.

"How long is the investigation supposed to take?" I asked.

"I don't know, but until you turn yourself in or end up dead, they'll probably never believe that we aren't working together. That little drone strike on the prison didn't help either because they're not believing the Middle Eastern confession. The CIA lost valuable assets and bargaining chips from different hostile countries that have American hostages. You leveled a fucking prison to kill one nigga, which was stupid and shortsighted."

"I'm sorry that you don't approve of my tactics, but just to be clear, I would've leveled a daycare center to get to that one nigga. He killed my mama and my sister, so he earned his place in hell, and not even God was gonna stand in my way on that issue," I stated boldly.

"So, what's you plan now, Nate? Kill me? I'm all you got left, bruh, so untie me, and we'll call it even for my fucking the shit out of Marissa."

"Call it even?" I asked, laughing aloud.

"Yeah, nigga! You acting like you're married to Marissa or in a relationship with her, but you're not, and that means she can do whatever she wants to do with her pussy. Including giving me some."

I didn't know if he was trying to get under my skin, but I wasn't about to let him provoke me into shooting him in the face just yet. The sound of the doorbell chiming was the perfect interruption.

"Ay, just hang out for a minute, and I'll be right back," I said, chuckling, as I moved past him.

I could hear him calling me every type of black Judas in the book, which was ironic considering that he was the one to betray my trust, but I ignored him and went upstairs to answer the door.

"How was your ride?" I asked, stepping aside to let her in.

"Shit, you already know that I slept the whole way. This pregnancy thing ain't no bitch," Joy replied, coming in.

"I'll take your word for it."

"Is that-Is that blood?" she asked, pointing to the red spots that stood in stark contrast to the white marble floor.

"I can explain."

"Nate, you muthafucka, get me down from here!" Stuckey yelled.

"Tell me that's not your brother's blood," she said, looking at me in disbelief.

I didn't answer. I simply took her by the hand and led her downstairs into the basement. As soon as she saw Stuckey's naked ass, she gasped and squeezed my hand at the same time.

"Nate, what the fuck?" she said in a fierce whisper.

"I promise that it'll all make sense in a second, just bear with me," I said, still holding onto her hand tightly.

"Joy, thank God you're here, so you can talk some sense into this nigga."

"Talk some sense into me? Well, here's some sense for your ass. Next time, don't think wit' your dick. I'll see you in hell, bruh," I said, pulling my gun out and shooting him twice in the heart.

"Oh, my God!" Joy yelled.

"Calm down and let me explain."

"There's *no* possible explanation for this shit, Nate! I mean, you just killed your own brother," she said, looking at me like I was the devil himself.

"Okay, yeah, I did do that, but I had a good reason so please just listen for a minute."

I waited for her to nod her head before I began to speak slowly and lay out my master plan for her. When I was finally done talking, she just stared at me with the most blank expression until her focus suddenly cleared up and locked in on me.

"You evil fucking genius," she said, chuckling uneasily.

"I know that it's a lot to take in, but this will work," I assured her.

"What about dental records?"

"Snatching out all of his teeth to make molds and crowns," I replied.

"Fingerprints?"

"Removed and grafted," I said, smiling.

"And what happens when they run DNA on the body to make sure?"

I pointed to the rather large bucket at my dead brother's feet.

"I'm gonna bleed him dry and shave him clean. I promise you that this will work because it's what the CIA wants to believe. It's what they *need* to believe," I said.

Before she could ask another plausible question, the doorbell rang, and I ran off to greet my other guest. When I came back downstairs with the doctor in tow, Joy was still standing in the same place, and I could smell electrical circuits burning because of how hard she was thinking.

"Joy, this is Doc."

When she turned around, he extended his hand, and out of polite reflex, she shook it.

"So, what is it that you're about to do?" she asked him.

"I'm gonna do what I did once before, and I'm gonna give Nathan a new face, or more accurately, I'm going to give him the face of this very dead gentleman here, and I'm gonna put Nate's old face on his dead body."

"Holy shit, this is real," she mumbled, moving to the chair that I'd occupied and sitting down swiftly.

"It's all perfectly safe, I assure you. When I'm done, I'll write you out a list and tell you all the things that you will need to do for his aftercare. Okay?" Doc asked her.

She nodded her head yes, but I could still see the shock in her eyes.

"Alright then. Nathan, shall we begin?" Doc asked, turning to me.

"I'm ready when you are," I replied, moving to grab the electric handsaw from my toolbox.

By the time I got back, I caught the sounds of a ringing phone suddenly going silent, and I looked to the two people in front of me for an explanation.

"It's not me," Joy said.

"It's not mine either," Doc added.

Before I could ask the next logical question, the buzzing sound of an incoming text message filled the room, and because I was standing right next to Stuckey's swinging body, I knew whose phone it was. I reached into his pocket, pulled it out, and used his thumb to unlock it. Seeing that the missed call was from none other than Marissa only made me feel more vindicated about my decision to kill this nigga, but when I opened the text from her and read it, I completely froze.

"Nate, what's wrong?" Joy asked.

I tried to open my mouth to explain, but I couldn't force the words out, so I simply passed her the phone.

"99.995% that Nate is..."

Her eyes immediately shot to mine, filled with fear and shock, as she let the phone fall from her fingers.

"You're my-You're my-You're my father," she whispered.

"Just breathe, Joy, it's gonna be okay," I said, trying to keep her calm.

"You're my-You're my..."

The next thing I knew, she was unconscious and slumped in the chair, and suddenly, life was way more than complicated...


2 Be Continued

## Lock Down Publications and Ca$h Presents
## Assisted Publishing Packages

*Due to an increase in the price of services we have increased our prices. The prices below reflect the price increase as of 11/1/24.*

| BASIC PACKAGE<br>$699<br>Editing<br>Cover Design<br>Formatting | UPGRADED PACKAGE<br>$1000<br>Typing<br>Editing<br>Cover Design<br>Formatting<br>Upload eBooks to Amazon<br>Upload Paperback to Amazon |
|---|---|
| ADVANCE PACKAGE<br>$1,400<br>Typing<br>Editing (line editing/content)<br>Cover Design<br>Formatting<br>Copyright Registration<br>Proofreading<br>Upload eBooks to Amazon<br>Upload Paperback to Amazon | LDP SUPREME PACKAGE<br>$1,700<br>Typing<br>Editing (line editing/content)<br>Cover Design<br>Formatting<br>Copyright Registration<br>Proofreading<br>Set up Amazon Account<br>Upload eBooks to Amazon<br>Upload Paperback to Amazon<br>Advertise on LDP's Amazon and Facebook Page |

***

Other services available upon request.
Additional charges may apply

**Lock Down Publications**
P.O. Box 944
Stockbridge, GA 30281-9998
**Phone:** 470 303-9761
**Email:** lockdownpublications@gmail.com

# Submission Guideline

Submit the first three chapters of your completed manuscript to ldpsubmissions@gmail.com. In the subject line add **Your Book's Title**. The manuscript must be in a Word Doc file and sent as an attachment. Document should be in Times New Roman, double spaced, and in size 12 font. Also, provide your synopsis and full contact information. If sending multiple submissions, they must each be in a separate email.

Have a story but no way to send it electronically? You can still submit to LDP/Ca$h Presents. Send in the first three chapters, written or typed, of your completed manuscript to:

**LDP: Submissions Dept**
P.O. Box 944
Stockbridge, GA 30281-9998

*DO NOT send original manuscript. Must be a duplicate.* Provide your synopsis and a cover letter containing your full contact information.

Thanks for considering LDP and Ca$h Presents.

# NEW RELEASES

BLOODLINE OF A SAVAGE 1-3
THESE VICIOUS STREETS 1-3
RELENTLESS GOON 1-3
**BY PRINCE A. TAUHID**

THE BUTTERFLY MAFIA 1-3
**BY FUMIYA PAYNE**

A THUG'S STREET PRINCESS 1&2
**BY MEESHA**

CITY OF SMOKE 3
**BY MOLOTTI**

GET IT IN SLUGS 1 &2
**BY B. STALL**

STANDING ON HER BUSINESS 1&2
**BY DG SANTANA**

STEPPERS 1,2&3
THE REAL BADDIES OF CHI-RAQ
**BY KING RIO**

THE LANE 1&2
**BY KEN-KEN SPENCE**

THUG OF SPADES 1&2
LOVE IN THE TRENCHES 2
CORNER BOYS
**BY COREY ROBINSON**

TIL DEATH 3
**BY ARYANNA**

DYING FOR LIKES 2 | ARYANNA

THE BIRTH OF A GANGSTER 4
**BY DELMONT PLAYER**

PRODUCT OF THE STREETS 1-3
**BY DEMOND "MONEY" ANDERSON**

NO TIME FOR ERROR
**BY KEESE**

MONEY HUNGRY DEMONS 1-2
**BY TRANAY ADAMS**

HUB CITY MENACE 1-3
**BY J. WHITE**

A THUGGISH PASSION 1&2
LAND OF DA HOOLIGANZ 1-4
KILLAZ ON STANDBY 1&2
**BY IRA B.**

FO'EVA ROLLIN 1&2
**BY ASSA RAYMOND BAKER**

THE LEVEL UP 1&3
**BY LUXURY KING**

# Coming Soon from Lock Down Publications/Ca$h Presents

IF YOU CROSS ME ONCE 6
ANGEL V
**By Anthony Fields**

A THUGS STREET PRINCESS 3
**By Meesha**

CORNER BOYS 2
**By Corey Robinson**

THA TAKEOVER
**By Keith Chandler**

BETRAYAL OF A G 2
**By Ray Vinci**

SAVAGE FAMILY EMPIRE 1&2
SOULLESS GOON 1,2&3
THE DIRTY SIDE OF MONEY 1,2&3
**By Prince**

FOR MY ENEMY'S SAKE
AMBITIONS OF A SLIDER
FRESH OFF DA PORCH
**By IRA B.**

THE TRUCKLOAD 1-4
TIPPIN' THE SCALES 1-3
BAD BITCHES WIT GUNZ 3
PROBLEM SOLVED 2
**By Christopher "Diesel" Hornezes**

# Available Now

RESTRAINING ORDER 1 & 2
By **CA$H & Coffee**

LOVE KNOWS NO BOUNDARIES 1-3
By **Coffee**

RAISED AS A GOON I, II, III & IV
BRED BY THE SLUMS I, II, III
BLAST FOR ME I & II
ROTTEN TO THE CORE I II III
A BRONX TALE I, II, III
DUFFLE BAG CARTEL I II III IV V VI
HEARTLESS GOON I II III IV V
A SAVAGE DOPEBOY I II
DRUG LORDS I II III
CUTTHROAT MAFIA I II
KING OF THE TRENCHES
By **Ghost**

LAY IT DOWN I & II
LAST OF A DYING BREED I II
BLOOD STAINS OF A SHOTTA I & II III
By **Jamaica**

LOYAL TO THE GAME I II III
LIFE OF SIN I, II III
By **TJ & Jelissa**

IF LOVING HIM IS WRONG…I & II
LOVE ME EVEN WHEN IT HURTS I II III
By **Jelissa**

PUSH IT TO THE LIMIT
By **Bre' Hayes**

BLOODY COMMAS I & II
SKI MASK CARTEL I, II & III
KING OF NEW YORK I II, III IV V
RISE TO POWER I II III
COKE KINGS I II III IV V
BORN HEARTLESS I II III IV
KING OF THE TRAP I II
By **T.J. Edwards**

WHEN THE STREETS CLAP BACK I & II III
THE HEART OF A SAVAGE I II III IV
MONEY MAFIA I II
LOYAL TO THE SOIL I II III
By **Jibril Williams**

A DISTINGUISHED THUG STOLE MY HEART I II & III
LOVE SHOULDN'T HURT I II III IV
RENEGADE BOYS 1-4
PAID IN KARMA 1-3
SAVAGE STORMS 1-3
AN UNFORESEEN LOVE 1-3
BABY, I'M WINTERTIME COLD 1-3
A THUG'S STREET PRINCESS 1&2
By **Meesha**

A GANGSTER'S CODE 1-3
A GANGSTER'S SYN 1-3
THE SAVAGE LIFE 1-3
CHAINED TO THE STREETS 1-3
BLOOD ON THE MONEY 1-3
A GANGSTA'S PAIN 1-3
BEAUTIFUL LIES AND UGLY TRUTHS
CHURCH IN THESE STREETS
By **J-Blunt**

CUM FOR ME 1-8
**An LDP Erotica Collaboration**

BLOOD OF A BOSS 1-5
SHADOWS OF THE GAME
TRAP BASTARD
By **Askari**

THE STREETS BLEED MURDER 1-3
THE HEART OF A GANGSTA 1-3
By **Jerry Jackson**

WHEN A GOOD GIRL GOES BAD
By **Adrienne**

THE COST OF LOYALTY 1-3
By **Kweli**

BRIDE OF A HUSTLA 1-3
THE FETTI GIRLS 1-3
CORRUPTED BY A GANGSTA 1-4
BLINDED BY HIS LOVE
THE PRICE YOU PAY FOR LOVE 1-3
DOPE GIRL MAGIC 1-3
By **Destiny Skai**

A KINGPIN'S AMBITION
A KINGPIN'S AMBITION II
I MURDER FOR THE DOUGH
By **Ambitious**

TRUE SAVAGE 1-7
DOPE BOY MAGIC 1-3
MIDNIGHT CARTEL 1-3
CITY OF KINGZ 1&2
NIGHTMARE ON SILENT AVE
THE PLUG OF LIL MEXICO 1&2
CLASSIC CITY
By **Chris Green**

A GANGSTER'S REVENGE 1-4
THE BOSS MAN'S DAUGHTERS 1-5
A SAVAGE LOVE 1&2
BAE BELONGS TO ME 1&2
A HUSTLER'S DECEIT 1-3
WHAT BAD BITCHES DO 1-3
SOUL OF A MONSTER 1-3
KILL ZONE
A DOPE BOY'S QUEEN 1-3
TIL DEATH 1-3
IMMA DIE BOUT MINE 1-6
DYING FOR LIKES
By **Aryanna**

A DOPEBOY'S PRAYER
By **Eddie "Wolf" Lee**

THE KING CARTEL 1-3
By **Frank Gresham**

THESE NIGGAS AIN'T LOYAL 1-3
By **Nikki Tee**

GANGSTA SHYT 1-3
By **CATO**

THE ULTIMATE BETRAYAL
By **Phoenix**

BOSS'N UP 1-3
By **Royal Nicole**

I LOVE YOU TO DEATH
By **Destiny J**

I RIDE FOR MY HITTA
I STILL RIDE FOR MY HITTA
By **Misty Holt**

LOVE & CHASIN' PAPER
By **Qay Crockett**

TO DIE IN VAIN
SINS OF A HUSTLA
By **ASAD**

BROOKLYN HUSTLAZ
By **Boogsy Morina**

BROOKLYN ON LOCK 1 & 2
By **Sonovia**

GANGSTA CITY
By **Teddy Duke**

A DRUG KING AND HIS DIAMOND 1-3
A DOPEMAN'S RICHES
HER MAN, MINE'S TOO 1&2
CASH MONEY HO'S
THE WIFEY I USED TO BE 1&2
PRETTY GIRLS DO NASTY THINGS
By **Nicole Goosby**

LIPSTICK KILLAH 1-3
CRIME OF PASSION 1-3
FRIEND OR FOE 1-3
By **Mimi**

TRAPHOUSE KING 1-3
KINGPIN KILLAZ 1-3
STREET KINGS 1&2
PAID IN BLOOD 1&2
CARTEL KILLAZ 1-3
DOPE GODS 1&2
By **Hood Rich**

THE STREETS ARE CALLING
By **Duquie Wilson**

STEADY MOBBN' 1-3
THE STREETS STAINED MY SOUL 1-3
By **Marcellus Allen**

WHO SHOT YA 1-3
SON OF A DOPE FIEND 1-4
HEAVEN GOT A GHETTO 1&2
SKI MASK MONEY 1&2
By **Renta**

GORILLAZ IN THE BAY 1-4
TEARS OF A GANGSTA 1/&2
3X KRAZY 1&2
STRAIGHT BEAST MODE 1&2
By **DE'KARI**

TRIGGADALE 1-3
MURDA WAS THE CASE 1-3
By **Elijah R. Freeman**

SLAUGHTER GANG 1-3
RUTHLESS HEART 1-3
By **Willie Slaughter**

GOD BLESS THE TRAPPERS 1-3
THESE SCANDALOUS STREETS 1-3
FEAR MY GANGSTA 1-5
THESE STREETS DON'T LOVE NOBODY 1-2
BURY ME A G 1-5
A GANGSTA'S EMPIRE 1-4
THE DOPEMAN'S BODYGAURD 1&2
THE REALEST KILLAZ 1-3
THE LAST OF THE OGS 1-3
By **Tranay Adams**

MARRIED TO A BOSS 1-3
By **Destiny Skai & Chris Green**

KINGZ OF THE GAME 1-7
CRIME BOSS 1-4
By **Playa Ray**

FUK SHYT
By **Blakk Diamond**

DON'T F#CK WITH MY HEART 1&2
By **Linnea**

ADDICTED TO THE DRAMA 1-3
IN THE ARM OF HIS BOSS
By **Jamila**

LOYALTY AIN'T PROMISED 1&2
By **Keith Williams**

YAYO 1-4
A SHOOTER'S AMBITION 1&2
BRED IN THE GAME
By **S. Allen**

TRAP GOD 1-3
RICH $AVAGE 1-3
MONEY IN THE GRAVE 1-3
CARTEL MONEY 1&2
By **Martell Troublesome Bolden**

FOREVER GANGSTA 1&2
GLOCKS ON SATIN SHEETS 1&2
By **Adrian Dulan**

TOE TAGZ 1-4
LEVELS TO THIS SHYT 1&2
IT'S JUST ME AND YOU
By **Ah'Million**

KINGPIN DREAMS 1-3
RAN OFF ON DA PLUG
By **Paper Boi Rari**

THE STREETS MADE ME 1-3
By **Larry D. Wright**

CONFESSIONS OF A GANGSTA 1-4
CONFESSIONS OF A JACKBOY 1-3
CONFESSIONS OF A HITMAN
CONFESSIONS OF A DOPE BOY
By **Nicholas Lock**

I'M NOTHING WITHOUT HIS LOVE
SINS OF A THUG
TO THE THUG I LOVED BEFORE
A GANGSTA SAVED XMAS
IN A HUSTLER I TRUST
By **Monet Dragun**

QUIET MONEY 1-3
THUG LIFE 1-3
EXTENDED CLIP 1&2
A GANGSTA'S PARADISE
By **Trai'Quan**

CAUGHT UP IN THE LIFE 1-3
THE STREETS NEVER LET GO 1-3
By **Robert Baptiste**

NEW TO THE GAME 1-3
MONEY, MURDER & MEMORIES 1-3
By **Malik D. Rice**

CREAM 2-3
THE STREETS WILL TALK
By **Yolanda Moore**

THE STREETS WILL NEVER CLOSE 1-3
By **K'ajji**

LIFE OF A SAVAGE 1-4
A GANGSTA'S QUR'AN 1-4
MURDA SEASON 1-3
GANGLAND CARTEL 1-3
CHI'RAQ GANGSTAS 1-4
KILLERS ON ELM STREET 1-3
JACK BOYZ N DA BRONX 1-3
A DOPEBOY'S DREAM 1-3
JACK BOYS VS DOPE BOYS 1-3
COKE GIRLZ
COKE BOYS
SOSA GANG 1&2
BRONX SAVAGES
BODYMORE KINGPINS
BLOOD OF A GOON
By **Romell Tukes**

CONCRETE KILLA 1-3
VICIOUS LOYALTY 1-3
BLOODY MONEY BAGS
By **Kingpen**

THE ULTIMATE SACRIFICE 1-6
KHADIFI
IF YOU CROSS ME ONCE 1-3
ANGEL 1-4
IN THE BLINK OF AN EYE
By **Anthony Fields**

THE LIFE OF A HOOD STAR
By **Ca$h & Rashia Wilson**

NIGHTMARES OF A HUSTLA 1-3
BLOOD AND GAMES 1&2
By **King Dream**

GHOST MOB
By **Stilloan Robinson**

HARD AND RUTHLESS 1&2
MOB TOWN 251
THE BILLIONAIRE BENTLEYS 1-3
REAL G'S MOVE IN SILENCE
By **Von Diesel**

MOB TIES 1-7
SOUL OF A HUSTLER, HEART OF A KILLER 1-3
GORILLAZ IN THE TRENCHES
OOPS CRY TOO 1&2
THE DAUGHTER OF A CARTEL BOSS
By **SayNoMore**

BODYMORE MURDERLAND 1-3
THE BIRTH OF A GANGSTER 1-4
By **Delmont Player**

FOR THE LOVE OF A BOSS 1&2
By **C. D. Blue**

KILLA KOUNTY 1-5
TENDER
By **Khufu**

MOBBED UP 1-4
THE BRICK MAN 1-5
THE COCAINE PRINCESS 1-10
STEPPERS 1-3
SUPER GREMLIN 1-4
A GANGSTA'S SON
By **King Rio**

MONEY GAME 1&2
By **Smoove Dolla**

A GANGSTA'S KARMA 1-5
By **FLAME**

KING OF THE TRENCHES 1-3
By **GHOST & TRANAY ADAMS**

BAD BITCHES WIT GUNZ 1&2
PROBLEM SOLVED
**By "Christopher Diesel" Hornezes**

QUEEN OF THE ZOO 1&2
By **Black Migo**

GRIMEY WAYS 1-3
BETRAYAL OF A G
By **Ray Vinci**

XMAS WITH AN ATL SHOOTER
By **Ca$h & Destiny Skai**

KING KILLA 1&2
By **Vincent "Vitto" Holloway**

BETRAYAL OF A THUG 1&2
By **Fre$h**

COUNTDOWN OF A KILLA 1&2
SEX, MURDER AND GOD 1&2
GUNS DOWN, BOTTOMS UP 1&2
**By Lo-Life**

THE MURDER QUEENS 1-7
By **Michael Gallon**

FOR THE LOVE OF BLOOD 1-4
By **Jamel Mitchell**

DYING FOR LIKES 2 | ARYANNA

HOOD CONSIGLIERE 1&2
NO TIME FOR ERROR
By **Keese**

PROTÉGÉ OF A LEGEND 1,2&3
LOVE IN THE TRENCHES 1&2
By **Corey Robinson**

THE PLUG'S RUTHLESS DAUGHTER 1&2
By **Tony Daniels**

BORN IN THE GRAVE 1-3
CRIME PAYS
By **Self Made Tay**

MOAN IN MY MOUTH
By **XTASY**

TORN BETWEEN A GANGSTER AND A GENTLEMAN
By **J-BLUNT & Miss Kim**

LOYALTY IS EVERYTHING 1-3
CITY OF SMOKE 1-3
By **Molotti**

HERE TODAY GONE TOMORROW 1&2
By **Fly Rock**

WOMEN LIE MEN LIE 1-4
FIFTY SHADES OF SNOW 1-3
STACK BEFORE YOU SPLURGE
GIRLS FALL LIKE DOMINOES
NAÏVE TO THE STREETS
By **ROY MILLIGAN**

PILLOW PRINCESS
By **S. Hawkins**

THE BUTTERFLY MAFIA 1-3
SALUTE MY SAVAGERY 1&2
By **Fumiya Payne**

THE LANE 1&2
By Ken-Ken Spence

THE PUSSY TRAP 1-5
By **Nene Capri**

DIRTY DNA
By **Blaque**

SANCTIFIED AND HORNY
by **XTASY**

# BOOKS BY LDP'S CEO, CA$H

TRUST IN NO MAN
TRUST IN NO MAN 2
TRUST IN NO MAN 3
BONDED BY BLOOD
SHORTY GOT A THUG
THUGS CRY
THUGS CRY 2
THUGS CRY 3
TRUST NO BITCH
TRUST NO BITCH 2
TRUST NO BITCH 3
TIL MY CASKET DROPS
RESTRAINING ORDER
RESTRAINING ORDER 2
IN LOVE WITH A CONVICT
LIFE OF A HOOD STAR
XMAS WITH AN ATL SHOOTER